At Home with Mr Darcy

Victoria Connelly

Cover image by Roy Connelly

Published by Cuthland Press
in association with Notting Hill Press

ISBN: 978-1-910522-02-8

www.victoriaconnelly.com

To my mother-in-law, Margaret, with love.

ACKNOWLEDGEMENTS

I would like to thank the following people who helped during the writing of this story: Erica James, Catriona Robb, and the staff at Chatsworth House and Lyme Park. Also, a special thank you to all the readers who love these characters as much as I do! I love reading your messages and hearing your thoughts.

* * *

'There is not a finer county in England than Derbyshire.'

Jane Austen, *Pride and Prejudice*

* * *

CHAPTER 1

There were books everywhere. They were on the tables, on the floor, on the stairs – there was even a pile on the washing machine which didn't bode well for when the spin cycle kicked in. Katherine Roberts – or Katherine Lawton as she now called herself in her private life – had never seen so many books and she was a lecturer at St Bridget's College in Oxford and was used to being surrounded by them.

'What are we going to do, Warwick?' she cried, her long dark hair looking somewhat dishevelled as she stood in the middle of the chaos.

'Don't worry,' Warwick said, emerging from the south-facing drawing room which was flooded with summer sunshine. 'It'll take a bit of sorting out but we'll get there.' He crossed the hallway to the living room where Katherine had been trying to uncover one of the sofas and took her face in his hands and kissed her. 'Hello, wife,' he said a moment later with a big grin.

'Hello, husband,' she said, melting instantly. It was almost a year since their wedding at Purley Hall in Hampshire and yet Katherine still felt like a newly-wed. Perhaps that was because it had taken them such a long time to find the perfect home.

Moving into Hawk's Hill Manor had been a much longer process than they'd anticipated what with solicitors moving in mysterious ways and the previous owner having a last-minute wobble as to whether she actually wanted to sell at all. But, finally, they'd exchanged contracts and the date had been fixed for the middle of July.

Set deep in beautiful Cotswold country to the north of Oxford, Katherine had agreed that it was worth the slightly longer commute into work than she had initially wanted because the Grade II listed Georgian property with its grand front door and nine sash windows was just too perfect. Katherine had almost cried when she'd first seen it.

'We can't afford this, Warwick,' she'd said.

'I think it's worth pushing the budget a little, don't you?' he'd said and she hadn't been able to put up any sort of a fight as she'd walked around the English country garden filled with topiary, lavender and roses and had admired the view across the sun-filled terrace from the breakfast room and the equally delightful views of gentle hills and verdant fields from each of the six bedrooms.

It was a sort of Purley Hall in miniature, Katherine had joked. Of course, it was far too big for just the two of them but Warwick had already been dropping hints that it wouldn't be just the two of them forever now, would it? One thing was for sure – it was the kind of home which was a real wrench to leave to go to work and Katherine had begun to envy Warwick being able to stay and work at Hawk's Hill each day, wandering through the sunny rooms and taking a turn about the garden like a Regency gentleman, surveying his perfect English acre.

The village was beautiful too, full of cottages built in the mellow gold stone that the Cotswolds was famous for. There was a ford by the church, a tiny shop with a post office counter, and a footpath leading to a quiet stretch of river which wound its way through the Oxfordshire countryside and gave Warwick and Katherine somewhere to jog together on weekend mornings.

The little cottage Katherine had lived in before was being rented out as unfurnished so all her worldly goods were now at Hawk's Hill. As were Warwick's from his home – The Old Vicarage – in West Sussex.

'I didn't realise we'd have so many things,' Katherine said to Warwick, rummaging once more through a tower of books which were in danger of spilling across the living room floor.

'It'll look better once everything's been put away,' Warwick said, idly picking up an ancient paperback with a cracked spine from the arm of a chair. 'Ah!' he said. 'I've been looking for this for *years!*'

One of the first things they'd done when they'd moved in was to employ a specialist carpenter who had made miles and miles of bookshelves for them in the two rooms they were to use as their studies as well as any other alcoves and neat recesses which would look all the better for being stuffed with books. Now, it was just a matter of sorting through their great collections and getting them into some sort of order.

Katherine believed that they needed at least half a mile of bookshelves for their Jane Austen titles alone as they both had each of the six novels in many different editions as well as the collections of the author's letters, juvenilia, and all the biographies and criticisms. And goodness only knew how many copies of *Pride and Prejudice* they now owned between them. It was quite mind-boggling.

Of course, there had been one truly heart-stopping moment when Warwick had been unpacking a box of books in his newly appointed study that did, in fact, belong to Katherine.

'Warwick!' she'd cried in alarm, her hair almost

standing on end.

Warwick had looked up from his task, thoroughly perplexed. 'What is it, Cherry?' he asked.

'They're *my* books!'

'Are they?'

Katherine had nodded and Warwick had taken out first one, then another, and then another.

'And so they are,' he'd declared, shaking his head and chuckling at his error.

But she hadn't remained cross with him for long. That was the thing about Warwick. He might have been extraordinarily good at getting himself into trouble but he was very adept at getting himself back out of it. Usually, he just needed to smile to make Katherine forget his maddening behaviour.

'You know, you just need to relax more,' he told her now. 'You expect everything to fall in to place straightaway and that isn't going to happen. Not with the timetables we've both had recently.'

Katherine nodded. Warwick was right, of course. He'd had yet another punishing deadline for a novel and had had two speaking engagements – one of which had taken him to Germany where he had a huge following for his racy Regency romances. Katherine had also been busy with the usual end of term turmoil at St Bridget's and had been collating notes for a series of essays she was writing to be published in academic journals.

'We need this break in Derbyshire,' he told her and Katherine smiled as she remembered their upcoming holiday. 'We've both been working so hard.'

Katherine nodded again. She was so looking forward to the trip. It was the first Purley Hall Jane Austen holiday – three glorious days in Derbyshire which was the county of Mr Darcy's ancestral home, Pemberley. Indeed, actress Dame Pamela Harcourt, who was overseeing the trip, had promised the Janeites not one Pemberley but *two* with trips to Chatsworth House in Derbyshire and a quick hop over the border to Lyme Park in Cheshire.

Katherine and Warwick had visited Derbyshire on a number of occasions but they had been rock climbing trips and, although they had both visited Chatsworth and Lyme on a number of occasions, they hadn't visited them together and, as any Austen addict knows, you can't have too many trips to Pemberley.

It was going to be hard to leave their home so soon after moving in even though they knew it would be in safe hands. Katherine had asked her dear friend Chrissie to come and cat sit for them and she'd leapt at the chance to stay at the beautiful manor house.

'No wild parties, mind,' Katherine had teased.

No, Katherine thought, she couldn't believe how lucky she was to live in such a beautiful house. They'd looked at a couple of much older houses whilst property hunting – one dating back to the fifteenth-century in parts but, after Warwick had hit his head for the sixth time on the low beams, they'd decided that their home would have to be Georgian. There'd never been any contest really for what Jane Austen fan could resist the pull of Georgian architecture?

She remembered that first magical viewing of Hawk's Hill when she'd walked into the living room and had imagined a roaring fire in the grand hearth and a Christmas tree sparkling in the corner. She'd gasped at the dining room and had known that it would be impossible to rush any meal there and dreamt of lingering over breakfast, sipping Earl Grey tea from a fine china cup. Then there'd been the terrace and the garden that was oh-so-perfect for summer parties with croquet, summer cocktails and strawberries and cream.

She watched Warwick bent double over a box full of orange-spined Penguin classics, his dark hair flopping across his face as he idly picked a title at random and mumbled something to himself as he thumbed through the pages. How much did she love this man? How lucky did she feel that he was her husband? As lucky as Elizabeth Bennet had felt when marrying Mr Darcy? Katherine smiled. Yes. She had found her Mr Darcy and her very own Pemberley too.

CHAPTER 2

Deep in the heart of the Hampshire countryside, tucked away in a corner of the Purley Hall estate, was Horseshoe Cottage. Its rosy red bricks, three windows and sweet porch over which clambered a great deal of honeysuckle made it look immediately warm and welcoming to any visitor.

The interior was no less welcoming with its squashy sofas, chintzy curtains and general feeling of being well lived-in and loved. It was the sort of home where you didn't worry too much if you walked in wearing a pair of wellies and where you were very likely to trip over a free-ranging chicken or sit on a dog who'd found the best seat in the house just before you had.

As with many country homes, the kitchen was where you could usually find its occupants and that was exactly where Dan and Robyn Harcourt were that morning.

'Are you *sure* you're going to be okay?' Robyn asked her husband as he rubbed a very wet Jack Russell Terrier named Biscuit with an old towel.

'Of course I'll be okay,' he said. 'I'm responsible for twelve horses now that the riding centre's up and running and these two dogs–'

'Yes but a toddler is a little bit different,' Robyn said. 'You can't just stick your daughter in a stable or bribe her with half a sausage like you can with Moby and Biscuit.'

'Oh, I don't know,' Dan said. 'It might be worth trying.'

'I do hope you're joking,' Robyn said. She was

sitting by the bright blue Aga with Cassie on her lap, brushing the curls that were so like her own but which were the same red-gold as Dan's hair.

Having decided that Biscuit was as dry as he could get him, Dan looked up and watched Robyn as she brushed Cassandra's hair.

'I can't believe she's almost two,' he said.

'I know,' Robyn said, kissing her daughter's cheek. 'The time's gone so quickly.'

'She'll soon be at school.'

'Don't say that!' Robyn said, unable to bear the thought of parting with her daughter so soon. Luckily, though, they had a primary school in Church Stinton so she wouldn't be too far away when the time came.

Dan crossed the room and scooped Cassandra up into his arms. 'Haven't you got to be heading up to the Hall?'

Robyn stood up and nodded. 'Yes. We're just tying up all the loose ends before tomorrow. Gosh, I do wish you were coming with us,' she said.

'So do I but somebody has to stay at home and take care of everyone.'

'And you're going to be brilliant at it, I'm sure,' Robyn told him. 'Did I tell you that Pammy asked if I wanted to do any of the spiels on the coach?'

'And what did you say?'

'I said I'd be absolutely petrified,' Robyn said with a laugh. 'Anyway, I wouldn't dream of stealing her limelight.'

'Yes, she does love that sort of thing,' Dan said. 'Give her a microphone and an audience and she's up and away.'

'I'm really looking forward to it,' Robyn said. 'Our first Jane Austen holiday! It's so exciting.'

'So, who's travelling up with you in the minibus?'

'Just Roberta and Rose who are coming through from Brighton. Everybody else is meeting us there,' she said.

'And the journalist?'

'She's booked in at the same hotel and is getting the train from London,' Robyn told him. 'What?' she asked, noticing the concerned look on his face.

'Do you trust her?'

'What you mean?' Robyn asked.

'I mean, she writes for *Vive!* – she's a journalist.'

'Well, I don't know her personally but I'm sure she'll do a good job.'

'Right,' Dan said.'

Robyn cocked her head to one side. 'What?'

'I'm just a bit worried about her. How do you know she's not going to do a hatchet job on you?'

Robyn laughed. 'Why would she be coming on a Jane Austen tour if she was just going to make fun of us?'

Dan gave her a pained look. 'Because that's what journalists like to do. They'll flatter you and make you think that they're your best friend and then they'll stab you in the back with their pen.'

'I don't think Melissa Berry is like that at all from what I've heard.'

Dan shook his head. 'Just keep an eye on her.'

'I have more than enough people to keep an eye on,' Robyn said. 'Mrs Soames is going to be there for a start.'

Dan laughed. 'I don't envy you that experience.'

Robyn sighed. 'I do wish she'd find some other interest. Perhaps we could persuade her to join another group. Maybe Charles Dickens or Thomas

Hardy have their own conferences. I think Mrs Soames would get on far better as a Thomas Hardy fan what with all those gloomy endings. I've never been able to understand how a woman who complains so much can really be a Jane Austen fan. Janeites are usually such happy people.'

'Maybe she's an impostor,' Dan suggested. 'Maybe she hasn't really read the books at all but just comes along to the conferences because she likes the costumes and dancing.'

'Oh, no,' Robyn said. 'She's a fan all right. She knows her stuff. You know, she's even bringing her daughter to Derbyshire. I wonder what she'll be like.'

'Blimey,' Dan said. '*Two* Mrs Soameses!'

Robyn's eyes doubled in size. 'I hope not. I really hope not.'

Dame Pamela Harcourt was hopeless when it came to packing even though she'd done her fair share of travelling over the years during her career as an actress. Then again, she didn't need to master the skill of the perfectly packed suitcase because she had Higgins the butler who always undertook the task himself.

'Madam, do allow me,' he'd say whenever he saw her flinging her expensive clothes in willy-nilly. Today, he was wearing a waistcoat in sky-blue with bright silver buttons which seemed to sing of summer and he had already taken charge of the luggage situation folding neatly and packing professionally.

'How many hats do you think I should take?' Dame Pamela asked him.

'A couple of wax rain hats should be just the thing,' Higgins said.

'Oh, don't be so pessimistic,' Dame Pamela chided him. 'We're going to have *glorious* summer weather, I just know it.' She thought back to the previous summer and the wedding of Katherine and Warwick and how, for a few dreadful hours, they'd thought that it was going to rain. But the sun had made a miraculous appearance and the gardens had been bathed in golden light. No, Higgins was most certainly not going to put a dampener on her first ever Jane Austen holiday.

'It's a truth universally acknowledged that the sun always shines for Janeites,' she said.

'Yes, madam,' Higgins said, clearly knowing when he was defeated.

'Now, back to my hats. I have a fabulous mint green summer hat somewhere with a large bow in the most ravishing shade of pink you've ever seen. That might be just the thing for Chatsworth.'

'Don't forget your walking boots, madam,' Higgins told her.

'Ah, yes,' Dame Pamela said, wrinkling her nose in disdain as she looked at the enormous boots. 'Dan assures me I'll need them for the Derbyshire countryside but I ask you, Higgins, do they really go with my dresses? I just can't see myself wearing them somehow.'

'One wouldn't like to twist one's ankle,' he said.

'No, I suppose not but that's exactly how Marianne Dashwood met the delectable Mr Willoughby.'

'Didn't that end badly?' Higgins asked, folding a silk blouse and placing it carefully into the suitcase. He hadn't ever admitted to reading or watching any Jane Austen but, having lived and worked with Dame

Pamela for so many years, it had been impossible not to pick up a certain amount of knowledge.

'Yes but she had such fun before all the heartache,' Dame Pamela said. 'Ladies do like the occasional rogue.'

Higgins shook his head. He would never understand the female heart.

'Maybe I could get away with a nice pair of canvas plimsolls,' Dame Pamela said a minute later. 'They'd certainly look more lady-like.'

'I think that would be a mistake, madam. I really think you should take the boots,' Higgins insisted.

'But just *look* at the colour! How very drab they are. Couldn't they make them in a more inspiring colour like pink or blue?' She shook her head. 'I suppose I'll just have to suffer in silence.'

Higgins cleared his throat. He'd never known his mistress to suffer in silence – it just wasn't in her make-up.

'And what will you do, Higgins, whilst I'm away?' she asked him.

'The silver needs polishing again,' he said, 'and I shall oversee the bookbinder when she arrives.'

'Of course,' Dame Pamela said, 'and I want you present when she handles our first edition of *Pride and Prejudice*.'

'Indeed, madam.'

Dame Pamela nodded. She had recently bought a rare first edition of Jane Austen's most famous novel at auction for the best part of two hundred thousand pounds. It was a purchase that had shocked even the most ardent Janeite but Dame Pamela hadn't been able to resist. After all, what was money for if not to be extravagant once in a while?

'I do hate leaving Purley but I'm so looking forward to this trip. I think it's going to be a resounding success, don't you?'

'Very likely, madam,' Higgins said.

'Just like the weddings.' She clasped her hands to her primrose-clad bosom. 'I can't believe that we've had five weddings here since Katherine and Warwick's. Word has certainly spread although I have to say I wasn't at all enamoured by that bride who wore that strapless, sleeveless gown. I thought she was going to spill right out of it when she bent over to cuddle that little bridesmaid. Honestly, I really must vet what brides are going to wear in the future. Purley has standards, after all.'

Higgins didn't say anything but he had blushed a deep crimson.

It was a bright summer's morning when the little white minibus pulled up outside Purley Hall. Dame Pamela refused point-blank to call it a minibus, however, because that was such an undignified name. In her books, it was a coach.

'Ah, Robyn,' she said, peering out of her study window. 'Do go and greet the driver, won't you? His name's Paul something or other.'

'Allsop,' Robyn said. 'Mr Allsop.'

Dame Pamela wasn't listening. She was rummaging through some of her coach spiel notes which were littering her desk. She was taking her role as a tour guide very seriously indeed.

Robyn walked down the great staircase and crossed the grand hallway, opening the front door to greet Mr Allsop who was standing scratching his head, neck craned up as he took in the house.

'Blimey!' he said. 'I never knew this was here.'

'Hello, Mr Allsop,' Robyn said, extending her hand to shake his. He was a small, thin man with a narrow face containing brilliant red cheeks and a pair of the brightest eyes Robyn had ever seen.

'You Dame Pamela, then?' he asked.

'Gracious, no,' Robyn said. 'I'm Robyn – her personal assistant. Dame Pamela will be down in a moment.' She smiled. Had this curious man really never heard of Dame Pamela Harcourt? She was one of the most famous actresses in England and a national treasure to boot.

'She own this place, then?'

'Yes,' Robyn said. 'She's an actress. Perhaps you've seen some of her films or plays?'

'Eh?' he said. 'Not me. I don't go in for much TV. Prefer a good book myself.'

'Then you should be in very fine company this weekend,' Robyn told him, 'for you'll be surrounded by book lovers.'

'So I've been informed. Jane Austen fans, isn't that right?'

Robyn nodded. 'That's right.'

'Yes, my second wife was all wrapped up in that Darcy nonsense.'

Robyn's eyes widened. 'Your second wife?'

He nodded. 'Divorced last year. Looking out for the third Mrs Allsop now.'

Robyn smiled. 'Come on in and have a cup of tea before we leave,' she said, wondering just how Mr Allsop would fare amongst a group of Janeites if he was a Darcy-basher.

Rose and Roberta had arrived in plenty of time and

were sitting in the garden at Purley Hall enjoying a glass of elderflower cordial and admiring the summer roses in the borders.

'I never tire of coming here,' Roberta said.

'I thought that incident with Dame Pamela's first edition of *Pride and Prejudice* might have put you off,' Rose said.

'It *wasn't* the first edition though, was it?'

'We didn't know that at the time,' Rose pointed out, remembering with a shudder what had happened during the Christmas conference.

'I must say, I can't help feeling a mite nervous every time I walk into a library now.'

'I'm not surprised,' Rose said. 'I can't take you anywhere, can I?'

Roberta gave a little chuckle. 'Goodness knows what will happen when they let me loose at Pemberley.'

'Which one?'

'*Both* of them,' Roberta said, thinking of the treats they had in store. 'I'm not sure I'll be able to take all the excitement! Just imagine being at home with Mr Darcy.'

Rose sighed. It had been her suggestion that they went on the first Purley Hall Austen holiday and she was beginning to wonder if she'd made a huge mistake.

Finally, after squashing yet more hats into a bag and being persuaded that she really didn't need her velvet cloak, Dame Pamela was ready to leave. Robyn had said a tearful goodbye to Dan and Cassie and had made her husband promise to ring her if anything – *anything* was to go wrong.

'What could *possibly* go wrong?' he'd said, bending his tall frame to kiss his wife, the light catching his red-gold hair. Robyn had had a little wobble. What was she thinking of – leaving like this?

It's only for a few days, she'd reminded herself and, with a final kiss on Cassie's rosy cheek, she'd joined Dame Pamela at the hall.

'Oh, Purley! My beloved Purley!' Dame Pamela cried dramatically, looking up at the towering splendour of the place she called home.

'I'm sure Dan and Higgins will take excellent care of everything,' Robyn assured her.

'Yes, yes, of course,' Dame Pamela said, batting her eyelashes as if blinking away tears. Robyn smiled. Dear Pammy would always be the actress, wouldn't she? Mind you, Robyn could feel tears vibrating in her own eyes.

'Ready?' she prompted.

'I suppose so,' Dame Pamela said and, in a rush of lilac chiffon, she boarded the minibus for the journey north.

CHAPTER 3

The Wye Hotel on the outskirts of Bakewell was a fine building made of a warm beige stone. Set back from the road and dating from the early nineteenth-century, its three storeys were both impressive and elegant with comfortable airy rooms overlooking landscaped gardens and the countryside of the Peak District beyond.

For the duration of their stay, the party from Purley Hall had the hotel to themselves which included all of the single, twin and double bedrooms, the dining room, a sitting room with a very impressive fireplace and enough books to keep even the most voracious reader happy, and another sitting room in which had been placed – at the special request of Dame Pamela – an array of comfortable chairs, a large television and DVD player.

'It's our own private room,' Mrs Baker, the owner of The Wye Hotel, had informed Dame Pamela when she'd asked if there were facilities for film nights.

'And very generous it is of you too,' Dame Pamela had told her, making a mental note to give her a framed signed photograph at the end of their stay. She always carried a few of them around with her wherever she went.

So, as Dame Pamela, Robyn, Rose and Roberta arrived, everything was set for the perfect weekend holiday. They only had to await the arrival of the other guests and they didn't have to wait long. Katherine and Warwick had driven up from the Oxfordshire countryside in Warwick's beloved Jaguar, and Mrs Soames had picked up by her daughter who lived in Doris Norris's Cotswold village and had given her a lift too. Both cars arrived within ten minutes of each other and Dame Pamela and Robyn were on hand to greet them.

'Katherine!' Robyn screamed when she saw her dear friend. They embraced warmly. 'How's the new house?'

'Old,' Katherine said with a smile. 'We have quite a bit of work to do on it but it's so beautiful. Promise me you and Dan will come to visit us soon? We have a gorgeous guest room and Cassie will adore the gardens.'

'We'd love to.'

'How's life at Purley?' Katherine asked.

'Busy, busy,' Robyn said. 'Always a wedding or a photo shoot or conference to prepare for. It's wonderful. And Dan's riding school is really taking off too.'

'That's brilliant,' Katherine said.

'Where's Warwick?' Robyn asked, looking around for Katherine's husband.

'Oh, he's promised to bring the bags in as soon as he's written something down. Inspiration struck him like a bolt of lightning as soon as we entered Derbyshire and he kept having to pull over to write.'

'He'll have to get a dictaphone,' Robyn said.

'He's too self-conscious,' Katherine explained. 'He doesn't like anyone to see his notes or his first drafts. He's very private that way.'

'And what's that like to live with?' Robyn asked. 'Do you mind at all?'

Katherine shook her head. 'As a fan of his books, I can't help wanting to sneak into his study and take a look at what he's up to. I've been really tempted a couple of times but I wouldn't dare because I know what it's like to work from home and I would hate anybody to betray my trust like that so I have to respect his wishes.'

'And you're happy at Hawk's Hill?'

Katherine beamed a smile. 'It's the most amazing place. I feel like a Jane Austen heroine wandering around the Georgian rooms. It's like living in a dolls' house.'

'It looks wonderful from the photographs you emailed us,' Robyn said. 'I can't wait to see it.'

They were rudely interrupted as the figure of Mrs Soames crashed through the front door into reception.

'Good heavens!' she exclaimed as soon as she was inside. 'This place was almost impossible to find. Could use a few more signposts,' she told the young lady behind the reception desk who blushed furiously. 'Lucky I didn't get lost although I'm surprised we didn't with my daughter's map reading skills.'

Katherine and Robyn exchanged knowing glances and then Robyn took a deep breath and stepped forward.

'Hello, Mrs Soames,' she said, a big bright smile fixed on her face. 'Have you thought about getting a Satnav? They're very useful.'

'And very expensive,' Mrs Soames said. 'What's wrong with a cheap road atlas?'

'But trying to read a road atlas makes me feel queasy,' a little voice piped from behind the great tank of Mrs Soames and Robyn noticed Mrs Soames' daughter for the first time. She was in her late forties and could only be described as mousy in terms of both looks and temperament. She had an expression on her face which suggested that she was permanently ill at ease with the world and yet there was a certain sweetness about her – a little light which danced somewhere in the depths of her hazel eyes.

'And she really did try her best,' Doris Norris said, stepping forward from where she too had been eclipsed by the enormous figure of Mrs Soames. 'Hello Robyn, dear.'

'Doris!' Robyn said, leaning forward to embrace her. 'How are you?'

'Can't complain,' she said with a tiny smile, her cheeks a perfect pink.

'No,' Robyn whispered, 'you leave that to somebody else, don't you?'

Doris cast her eyes to the ceiling and Robyn shook her head in understanding. She did not envy Doris Norris her journey to Derbyshire.

'Mrs Soames is *not* a natural driver,' Doris whispered to Robyn as Mrs Soames continued her tirade against life to the poor young girl on reception. 'She was forever pumping that brake and I'm sure we must have done at least six emergency stops. I think my neck might be out of joint.'

'Oh, dear,' Robyn said. 'Well, let's get you settled into your room and make you a nice cup of tea.'

'Actually, I was hoping there might be a minibar,' Doris said with a little giggle.

'I'm not sure there is,' Robyn said, 'but I'm sure we could get you a little tipple from the hotel's bar. Just leave it with me.'

'What a sweetheart you are,' Doris said, clasping Robyn's hands in hers.

'And you must be Annie?' Robyn said, stepping forward. 'I'm Robyn. We spoke on the phone.'

'How lovely to meet you at last,' Annie Soames said, shaking Robyn's hand and giving her a lovely warm smile which lit up her pale face.

'Anne!' her mother barked, turning around. 'Bring those bags.'

'Yes, Mother,' Annie said.

'Poor girl,' Doris said to Robyn. 'She's been barked at for the whole of the journey.'

Robyn shook her head. 'Imagine having been brought up by Mrs Soames,' she said, giving a little shiver.

It was then that a young woman walked into the hotel reception. She was carrying a neat red suitcase in one hand and a laptop in the other. It could only be one person: Melissa Berry the journalist. She was in her mid-twenties and had short dark hair that was cut in a flicky elfin style and her dark eyes were heavily made up with thick eyeliner and false eyelashes that gave her a sort of Bambi look only without the innocence for she had a sharp look.

She clocked Robyn straightaway and, putting her things down, strode across the reception, her manicured hand extended in greeting.

'Melissa Berry,' she said. 'With *Vive!*.'

'Good to meet you,' Robyn said, her hand being mercilessly pumped. 'I'm Robyn.'

'Ah!' Dame Pamela suddenly surged forward. 'Ms Berry.'

'Dame Pamela,' Melissa said with a smile which Robyn didn't quite trust. There was something at the edge of it – something which hinted at mockery.

'I trust you will be comfortable here,' Dame Pamela said, 'and that you're looking forward to finding out what it's like to be true Janeite.'

'Indeed I am,' Melissa said.

'Well, we'll let you get settled in. Dinner will be at seven o'clock and then you can join us for the quiz.'

'The quiz?'

'Yes, we're hoping you'll join in,' Dame Pamela said, laughing at the startled look on the young journalist's face.

'I don't really know that much about Jane Austen,' Melissa confessed.

'Well, you will after this weekend,' Dame Pamela told her.

CHAPTER 4

Everybody was looking forward to the quiz. Except Melissa Berry. She had found it hard to understand why everybody was getting so excited. Quizzes were dull and boring, weren't they? She really didn't see the point in them. Still, it would give her a good opportunity to do what she was good at: people watch. So, with her notepad in hand, she headed into the sitting room.

It was a comfortable enough sort of a room but the little party found it hard not to miss the grandeur of the library at Purley Hall with its shelves of magnificent books, the warm glow from its lamps and candles and the attentive presence of Higgins the butler. Still, it looked jolly enough and lots of little tables had been put out for them at Robyn's request.

'Into pairs, everybody,' Dame Pamela announced as Robyn handed out Purley Hall paper to everybody together with brand new pens which they'd had made featuring a beautiful black and white image of Purley.

'Can we keep these, dear?' Doris Norris asked.

'Yes, they're yours,' Robyn said.

'How lovely,' Doris said.

'I hope they don't leak,' Mrs Soames said, clicking hers on and off repeatedly and peering hard at the nib. 'I once had a ghastly experience with a pen in my handbag – leaked all over that nice lace handkerchief from Stow on the Wold, remember, Anne?'

'Yes, Mother,' Annie said. 'I remember.'

Everybody had got into pairs. There was Katherine and Warwick, Mrs Soames and Annie, Rose, Roberta and Doris who were allowed to form a group of three as Robyn couldn't make up a pair as she'd helped Dame Pamela to set the questions.

'Melissa!' Robyn called across the room. 'Come and join us.'

Melissa looked up from where she was sitting scribbling in her notepad, gave a weak smile and got up.

'What do you think she was writing?' Doris asked.

'Probably just making notes about the hotel,' Robyn said, 'and what we're all up to.'

Joining them at their little table, Melissa cleared her throat.

'I'm afraid I'm not likely to help much,' she said, 'I don't know a single thing about Jane Austen.'

'You don't need to, dear,' Doris said. 'You're amongst true Janeites here.'

'I keep hearing that word, *Janeite*,' Melissa said. 'Is that something you made up yourselves?'

'Good gracious, no!' Doris exclaimed. 'It's been around since the 1890's, hasn't it, Robyn?'

'That's right. It was first used in an introduction to *Pride and Prejudice* by somebody called George Saintsbury. It's rather good, isn't it?'

'Hmmmm,' Melissa said, sounding unconvinced. 'Surely Austenite would be better?'

'We sometimes call ourselves Austen Addicts,' Robyn said, 'but never Austenites. Janeite is much more–' she paused, 'familiar, don't you think? We all feel very close to our favourite author, you see. So it would be strange to refer to her as Austen all the time.'

Melissa nodded, her eyes narrowed as if in concentration.

'I think we're about to begin,' Doris said as Dame

Pamela held her hands up for silence.

'Good evening, everyone,' she said. 'After that lovely dinner, how splendid it is to have this room at our disposal for our little quiz. Now, have we all got paper and pens? Good. Because I have a very special quiz for you tonight. Owing to our surroundings, I have devised some very special Derbyshire-based questions for you,' Dame Pamela announced.

There were a few murmurs of approval from around the room.

'So, are we ready to begin?' she asked. 'Question one: Elizabeth is joining the Gardiners on their trip to Derbyshire but where had they originally hoped to visit?'

From the other side of the room, Katherine leaned in towards Warwick. 'The Lake District, she whispered.

'Although it's just referred to as "the Lakes",' Warwick said and Katherine nodded, jotting the answer down in her neat handwriting.

'Question two: name any two real-life places which the party pass through en route to Derbyshire,' Dame Pamela said.

From the amber-coloured sofa near the French doors, Roberta looked at Rose. 'I think they mentioned Oxford,' she said.

Rose nodded. 'I'm pretty sure Blenheim was mentioned too.'

'Put those down, then – they sound about right,' Roberta said.

'Number three,' Dame Pamela said. 'When Mr Darcy and Elizabeth are talking in the grounds of Pemberley, which two places do they discuss with "great perseverance"?'

'Oh, that's Matlock and Dovedale,' Rose said to Doris.

'I shall trust you on that one,' Doris said. 'My memory isn't what it once was.'

'Number four,' Dame Pamela said. 'Chatsworth House is, of course, used as Pemberley in the 2005 film adaptation staring Keira Knightley but which other film did Ms Knightley star in which was filmed at Chatsworth?'

'Too easy!' Mrs Soames declared, shaking her head in dismay as she wrote the title 'The Duchess' onto her piece of paper, not bothering to confer with her daughter about it.

The questions continued with some fiendishly difficult ones about the county of Derbyshire itself that had everybody in the room scratching their heads, and then the quiz was over and everyone wrote their team names at the top of their answer sheet and handed them to Dame Pamela and, whilst she marked them, tea and coffee was served.

Melissa was fidgeting in her chair, her pen in the corner of her mouth as she observed everybody. After the quiz had finished, she'd sneaked off to the hotel bar and had come back with a gin and tonic.

'How you do guys *know* all this stuff?' she asked Doris Norris.

Doris chuckled. 'We spend far too much of our lives with our heads stuck in a book.'

'That isn't such a bad thing, though,' Robyn pointed out. 'Don't forget that Mr Darcy believed that a woman could only improve herself with "extensive reading".'

'That's right,' Doris said.

'That's a quote, right?' Melissa asked.

'From *Pride and Prejudice*,' Robyn said. 'Have you read it?'

'I skimmed it very quickly to get the gist for the piece I'm writing,' Melissa said. 'I watched some of the film with Keira Knightley but I didn't see the end.'

'Why not?' Doris asked, her forehead creasing.

'It really wasn't my kind of thing,' she said.

'But you didn't give it a chance,' Doris said.

'It just seemed to be one dull dance scene after another.'

Doris's eyes widened in horror. 'Dull?'

'Forgive me for asking but why did you volunteer to come away with us?' Robyn asked. 'I mean, if you're not really interested in all this.'

Melissa stared at Robyn for a moment as if she was wondering if it was wise to answer the question. Then she took a sip of gin and tonic and shrugged.

'I just needed to get out of the office for a bit.' It was then that Melissa's phone rang. 'Excuse me,' she said, standing up and leaving the sitting room.

'Now, there's a young woman in need of Jane Austen if ever I met one,' Doris Norris said and Robyn nodded in agreement, watching as Doris leaned across in her chair to where Melissa Berry had left her notebook.

'Doris! What are you doing?' Robyn asked in horror.

'Oh, just taking a little look,' Doris said.

'You really shouldn't be doing that.'

'I guess not,' Doris said, 'because I left my glasses in my room.'

Robyn shook her head and anxiously looked towards the foyer where Melissa was still on the phone, shouting at somebody.

'Robyn?'

'Yes?'

'What does *nescient* mean?' Doris asked, squinting at the page before her.

'Erm, I'm not sure,' Robyn said.

Doris looked across the room. 'Psssst! Katherine!'

Katherine looked up from her cup of tea as Doris motioned her over.

'Doris!' Robyn cried, anxious that Melissa would return at any moment.

'Katherine, dear – what does "nescient" mean?'

'It means a lack of knowledge. Ignorance. Why?'

'Oh, dear,' Doris said.

'What is it?' Robyn asked.

'That's how she's described us,' Doris said.

Katherine took the notebook from Doris and scanned it before sighing. 'Is this the reporter's?' she asked.

Doris and Robyn nodded.

'Then we're in trouble.'

It was then that Melissa strode back into the room. Robyn quickly grabbed the notebook from Katherine and returned it to Melissa's chair just in time.

'Everything okay?' Melissa asked as Katherine quickly returned to her seat next to Warwick.

'Yes, yes.' Robyn said. 'Just getting up for a stretch. I've been sitting down too long today.'

'Me too,' Doris said. 'My old bones need to get up and about every so often otherwise they'll seize up.' She did a funny little jig and Melissa's eyebrows rose a fraction. Luckily, Dame Pamela distracted them with a clap of her diamond-encrusted hands.

'Does she always wear so much jewellery?' Melissa

asked.

'Always,' Doris said. 'Wonderful, isn't it? She's like Elizabeth Taylor only with a little more class.'

Robyn giggled. Doris Norris could be ever so naughty sometimes.

'I now have the results of the quiz and a very good job you all did too. It was pretty close but we have a definite winner with an incredible twenty out of twenty.' Dame Pamela paused, holding up a hand and making sure she had everybody's undivided attention. 'And the winning team is,' she said, pausing again for dramatic effect, 'Soames on the Roam! That's Mrs Soames and her daughter, Annie.'

There was a big round of applause and Mrs Soames deigned to smile but it was so brief that it could have just been a facial twitch.

'You see, Mother,' Annie said, 'I told you Mother Shipton's cave wasn't in Derbyshire.'

'What are you talking about, girl? I never said that,' Mrs Soames said, her great bosom rising in defence. Annie rolled her eyes.

'Congratulations, ladies,' Dame Pamela said, moving forward to shake their hands. 'You will, of course, be receiving signed photos of me in my role as Marianne Dashwood in my heyday and I have gift vouchers for you here to spend at Chatsworth House tomorrow.'

Mrs Soames snatched the vouchers from Dame Pamela.

'I'd better take care of these,' she said to Annie. 'You always lose things.'

'I don't always lose things,' Annie said, taking a sip of tea to try and calm herself. This, she thought, was going to be a very long weekend. She'd dreamt of visiting Chatsworth House and Lyme Park – the two Pemberleys – for years but she was beginning to wonder if a weekend spent in her mother's company was too high a price to pay.

Out in the foyer, Robyn, Doris, Katherine and Warwick were in deep discussion about Melissa Berry's notepad.

'What else had she written?' Robyn asked.

Katherine frowned as she tried to remember. 'She said that Jane Austen has had her time and that people should be focussing on modern writers now – writers who have something to say about the world we live in.'

Warwick scoffed. 'But Jane Austen is still relevant today. I bet this woman would say the same thing about Shakespeare and Dickens. Just because they were writing in a different century doesn't mean they're outdated and have nothing to teach us.'

'Of course,' Katherine said. 'We all know that and it's something I always try to remind my students of too but it seems that this journalist is very set in her ways.'

'It seems like she's written her article on us already,' Warwick said, shaking his head.

'Dan warned me about this,' Robyn confided.

'Did he?' Doris said.

Robyn nodded. 'He said we're easy targets and that we really shouldn't have courted the press at all but Pammy was delighted at the idea of a journalist coming along with us.'

'Ah,' Katherine said, 'this may come back to haunt her.'

'We've got to warn everyone,' Robyn said. 'Don't

you think? I mean, we can't just sit back and do nothing, can we?'

'But what can we do?' Doris asked. 'The girl's obviously made her mind up about us.'

A little smile spread itself across Robyn's face. 'We'll just have to *un*make her mind up, won't we? I mean, there are more of us than there are of her and we've got the whole weekend ahead of us.'

Warwick grinned. 'Robyn's right. Miss Berry is surrounded by some of the most ardent Janeites in England. If *we* can't change her mind about Austen then nobody can.'

CHAPTER 5

The next morning before breakfast, Robyn filled Dame Pamela in on the discovery about Melissa Berry.

'Are you sure?' Dame Pamela asked. 'Are you *absolutely* sure?'

'Pretty sure,' Robyn said. 'Katherine and Doris saw the notes she'd made. They weren't very flattering.'

'Oh, dear,' Dame Pamela said. 'I feel so responsible.'

'Don't blame yourself,' Robyn said kindly. 'You weren't to know.'

'But I should have. I *really* should have,' Dame Pamela said, shaking her head in dismay. 'I never seem to learn my lesson with journalists. Each time, they win me over with flattery and then betray me!'

'That's not true,' Robyn said. 'You've had some wonderful pieces written about you.'

When Robyn had taken on the role of personal assistant to Dame Pamela, she had been given the rare privilege of looking through the vast archives of clippings which had been kept over the decades to get her up to speed. It had to be said that there were a few stinkers of reviews for some of the theatre performances and films but that was to be expected in any career which spanned the years as Dame Pamela Harcourt's had but, for the most part, they were glorious. The public and the press adored her.

'But what are we going to do?' Dame Pamela said, twisting an enormous diamond solitaire on her left hand.

'I think we should call a meeting,' Robyn said. 'We

should let everybody know what's going on because Melissa Berry is going to write about us all, isn't she?'

Dame Pamela nodded. 'Yes, yes,' she said.

'Now, I saw Melissa head into Bakewell. She said she going in search of a proper cup of coffee.'

'What's wrong with the coffee here?' Dame Pamela asked.

'Not up to her London standards, obviously,' Robyn said, 'but that'll buy us some time. I'll round everybody up and we can take it from there.'

Dame Pamela took a deep, fortifying breath and Robyn could see that she had instantly regained her composure after her initial scare. They were going to fight this together, Robyn thought.

Just ten minutes later, the little group of holidaying Janeites had gathered in the living room.

'I knew she wasn't to be trusted,' Mrs Soames said, her chin wobbling as she shook her head.

'How did you know that?' Rose asked. 'She seemed like a perfectly decent girl to me.'

'She's from London, isn't she?' Mrs Soames said. 'You can't trust anyone from London.'

Annie shook her head in despair at her mother's generalisation.

'But how are we going to stop her from writing what she wants?' Roberta asked.

'What do you mean, how do we stop her?' Dame Pamela said. 'We've got to make her fall in love with Jane Austen – *that's* how! And that can't be hard for a group as passionate as we are.'

'But is that morally right?' Rose asked.

'Who cares if it's morally right or not when the reputation of Jane Austen and her fans are on the line?' Dame Pamela said and there were a few nods of agreement from around the room.

Robyn cleared her throat and chipped in. 'What I think we should do is to expose Melissa Berry to the very best that Jane Austen has to offer.'

'Indeed!' Dame Pamela said. 'The most moving scenes from the books and the films, the most passionate declarations of love, the heights that the human heart can soar to and the depths of despair that her characters feel,' Dame Pamela said, making it sound – once again – as if she was reading from a very well-rehearsed script.

Everybody listened in stunned silence.

'Any ideas, anyone?' Robyn asked when she was quite sure Dame Pamela had finished.

'Emma Thompson's crying scene in *Sense and Sensibility*,' Roberta suggested.

'Yes but you have to build up to it – you can't just fast forward to it – you have to experience the whole thing and I'm not sure we've time for that as we've got to prioritise *Pride and Prejudice* on this trip,' Robyn said.

'Captain Wentworth's letter to Anne – I could read that to her,' Rose offered.

'And we certainly have time to watch the whole of the 2005 *Pride and Prejudice* again,' Doris Norris said. 'She simply *has* to melt after that.'

Suddenly, everybody was talking at once, swapping ideas and exchanging plans.

'She's a wordsmith,' Warwick said. 'She's bound to appreciate that famous passage from *Northanger Abbey* about novels. I'll see if I can wiggle that into a conversation with her.'

'I'm not sure I want you wiggling anywhere near

that journalist,' Katherine said, looking alarmed.

'And we can tell her about the life Jane led and how she turned down a marriage proposal and stayed true to herself and her art,' Mrs Soames said gravely.

'And how the world lost her when she was much too young,' Doris Norris said, shaking her head ruefully.

'Shush! She's coming,' Robyn said, sounding the alarm. Everybody moved at once, crashing into each other in an attempt to look natural.

Melissa Berry eyed them warily as she entered the living room of the Wye Hotel. She might have thought them a complete bunch of crazies but she had absolutely no idea what they had planned for her.

Horseshoe Cottage felt strange without Robyn, Dan thought as he tidied up the kitchen having fed Cassie her breakfast and handed her over to her babysitter for the day. He hated not being able to take care of her but he had a business to run now. The Purley Hall Riding Centre had been up and running for almost a year with a book full of regular pupils from pony-mad girls in pink jodhpurs to adults wanting to improve their technique. There was also a party of special needs children who came once a week to build their confidence on the quieter horses. Dan adored teaching them. He got such great satisfaction seeing the smiles on their faces.

Then there was Jack, the young man who was desperately trying to learn to ride in time for his wedding next year when he wanted to surprise his fiancée by riding into the reception venue. The only trouble was, he had no natural skill at all when it came to riding. Dan had given him a leg up onto Gemini –

one of the more docile ponies in the yard – and he'd promptly fallen off the other side. Luckily, he hadn't been hurt. Only his pride had been dented a little and Dan had had the good grace not to laugh.

Business, he thought as he strode up the driveway of Purley Hall towards the stable yard, was good. He now found it hard to imagine any other life for himself and would often reflect on his days spent working in the city of London, trapped in an office with wall-to-wall meetings, suffering eyestrain and headaches. No, he thought, he was one lucky man to be living and working in the beautiful Hampshire countryside with his dear family.

Entering the yard, he inhaled deeply, luxuriating in that wonderful smell of horse, hay and leather. He rolled up the sleeves of his checked shirt, revealing arms that were already tanned as well as toned, and got to work cleaning out the stables. It was a job that he could easily have left for one of the girls they employed but Dan had never been one to shirk physical work and he enjoyed working up a bit of a sweat. There were twelve horses to take care of now including one that had come to them in the strangest of manners.

Last winter, the skinniest of horses had been found tied to a gate on the Purley estate. There'd been an envelope fixed to the rope and, inside, had been a hastily written note.

'Plese look arfter this hors.'

No other explanation. Dan had asked around the village but nobody seemed to know anything about the poor abandoned animal.

'What are we to do with it?' Dame Pamela had asked on meeting the nervous piebald for the first time. 'It's in poor condition. Maybe we should ring the RSPCA or find a retirement home for her.'

Dan had shaken his head. 'She was brought *here*, Pammy,' he said. 'To *us*. Don't you think we should take her in?'

Dame Pamela hadn't needed much persuasion and Dan had got to work on the animal. They'd called her Winter. She was a nervous little cob and Dan began to wonder if she'd been mistreated. She was terrified of their Jack Russell, Biscuit, which was a real problem as he loved to run around the stables sniffing out rats so Dan did his best to keep Biscuit away from her and, slowly but surely, the horse began to trust him, letting him approach her and allowing him to stroke her neck with a friendly hand.

Winter had been left in her stable that morning because Dan wanted to keep an eye on a tiny wound which he'd found on her back.

'There now,' he said as he slowly entered with a carrot. Winter took it from him and he listened to the happy sound of a horse munching. He took the opportunity to look at the little wound and was pleased to see that it was healing nicely.

'We'll get you out in the field,' he said, opening the stable door and leading her into the yard.

It was just then that a pair of pigeons landed, flying down from the clock tower. They were the pigeons which Biscuit usually loved to chase but Dan was still wary about having the little terrier in the yard at the same time as Winter and so had left Biscuit at home. However, even without the dog there, the fluttering wings of the pigeons had just the same effect on the nervous horse who immediately reared up, neighing loudly before trying to bolt, catching

Dan in the shins with a pair of flying feet.

He dropped the leading rein and collapsed into himself in agony.

'Winter!' he cried but there was absolutely nothing he could do as the horse galloped out of the stable yard.

CHAPTER 6

'Chatsworth is one of England's greatest "Treasure Houses",' Dame Pamela announced as the minibus came to a halt after arriving at its first Pemberley, 'and a place I was lucky enough to call home for a summer whilst I was filming *Twelfth Night*.' She paused as the minibus exploded into applause as everybody remembered the *tour de force* that was Dame Pamela's Viola.

'Pemberley was thought to be situated near Bakewell,' she continued, 'and many Jane Austen fans believe that Chatsworth is the house she had in mind when she was envisioning Mr Darcy's home.' She took a deep breath. ' "To Pemberley, therefore, they were to go." '

Everybody except Melissa cheered as they remembered the line from the book, standing up from their seats and grabbing their bags and cameras.

'This is too too exciting!' Doris Norris exclaimed as she caught Katherine's eye.

'You know, Elizabeth and the Gardiners took "their Northern tour" in the month of July. So we're here at the perfect time too,' Katherine said.

'Of course,' Dame Pamela said. 'We like to get things right, you know.'

'Isn't it Chatsworth on the front of the Hodder edition of *Pride and Prejudice*? I'm sure it is,' Annie said, producing a copy from her handbag.

'It looks very much like it,' Rose said, peering at it.

Mr Allsop, the driver, cleared his throat. 'Can I switch this off now?' he asked.

Dame Pamela looked confused for a moment and

then she realised that the Dario Marianelli soundtrack to the 2005 film adaptation was still playing.

'Oh, yes,' she said.

'Thanks heavens for that,' he said under his breath.

Dame Pamela shot him a look of disapproval as she left the minibus.

The driver turned to look at Robyn. 'You folks really are nuts about this Austen woman, aren't you?'

'Oh, yes,' Robyn said.

They were to spend the entire day at Chatsworth. With the enormous house, extensive gardens and grounds as well as the restaurant, cafes and deluxe shops to be visited, there was enough to entertain any holidaymaker let alone a Janeite who needed to do nothing more than wander around with a trusty copy of *Pride and Prejudice* in their hands.

The group soon split up with most making a beeline for the house first. Robyn was one of them, drifting around in a dream as her eyes roamed from fine old portraits to decadent pieces of furniture. She gloried in crossing the black and white floor in the Painted Hall just as Keira Knightley had done in the 2005 adaptation, and nearly screamed for joy when she saw her first view of the Emperor Fountain from one of the bevelled glass windows.

It was an enormous house with so many splendid rooms that it made Robyn feel quite dizzy. Like Elizabeth Bennet when she visited Pemberley, Robyn made sure she looked out of each window at the landscape beyond, glorying in the immaculate gardens and the countryside in which they were set.

' "To be mistress of Pemberley might be something!" ' she quoted to herself, remembering Elizabeth's words as she'd thought about what her future might have been had she accepted Mr Darcy's first proposal. Robyn smiled. How would she have reacted if Dan had revealed himself to be the master of a property like Pemberley? Would she have swooned at the thought of being its mistress? She didn't think so. She probably would have run a mile because their home at Horseshoe Cottage was her idea of perfection. Of course, she was also lucky enough to be able to work at Purley Hall which was grand by anybody's standards. No, she thought, as beautiful as they were, the Chatsworths and Pemberleys of the world were suited to other people – not her.

After touring the house, Katherine and Warwick found themselves walking behind Melissa Berry. She had shunned the house in favour of the gardens and was now making her way towards the stable block where the restaurant and shops were.

'Shall I tackle her now?' Warwick asked Katherine.

'I don't like your use of the word *tackle*,' Katherine said. 'It sounds like you're going to get her in some sort of head lock.'

'I wish I could,' he said, 'then maybe I could make her see reason.'

'You haven't got to make her see reason,' Katherine said, 'only the joys of Jane Austen.'

'Isn't that the same thing?' Warwick asked with a lopsided smile that still melted Katherine. 'Leave her to me. You go and buy yourself a book or something in the shop.'

Katherine laughed. 'I don't need any encouragement to buy books.'

They entered a wide courtyard where tables and

chairs were set out and people were eating and drinking in the sunshine. There was a small fountain in the middle and a bar at the far side selling drinks and ice creams. Melissa Berry was heading towards the bar.

'Can I get you a coffee?' Warwick asked as he approached her.

She jumped in alarm. 'I thought you lot would all be in the house following in the footsteps of Mr Darcy,' she said.

'We've just been round,' he said.

They both bought coffee and went to sit on a couple of the bright purple seats.

'How long have you been a journalist?' he asked.

'A couple of years,' she said, sipping her coffee.

'And you like it?'

'Sure,' she said. 'Do you like being a novelist?'

'So you know about that?'

'It's my business to know about the people I write about,' she said, her face blank and unreadable. 'So, do you like it?'

'I love it,' he said. 'It's the kind of job you couldn't do unless you love it.'

'I guess,' she said and there was a pause.

'So,' Warwick began again after taking a sip of his coffee, 'have you read much Jane Austen?'

'No,' Melissa said bluntly. 'Just a bit of that *Pride and Prejudice* one and some stuff about her life in preparation for this job.'

Warwick's left hand clenched into an angry fist under the table. *A bit of that Pride and Prejudice one*. She was a hopeless case, wasn't she?

'There's something I want you to hear,' he said, carrying on regardless as he took a paperback copy of

Northanger Abbey out of his pocket.

'You carry that around with you all the time?' Melissa asked, an eyebrow raised in disbelief.

'I like to have something decent to read on me at all times,' he said. Well, he wasn't going to confess to having popped it in his pocket that very morning with the express purpose of reading her an extract, was he?

'Okay,' she said. 'What are you going to read me?'

'It's a passage I've always appreciated as a writer and I thought you might like it too,' he said. 'It's the perfect response to anybody who belittles the work of a novelist.'

'And you've had your work belittled?' Melissa asked, leaning forward slightly.

'Of course,' Warwick said. 'When you write books for as many years as I have, you have to take the bad reviews along with the good. But you'll know that as a journalist, won't you? I mean, you'll have had to have reported something – told a story – that upset somebody.'

'Absolutely,' she said matter-of-factly.

'Then I think you'll appreciate this,' he said, opening the book at the relevant page which he'd dog-eared. A habit which drove Katherine nuts.

'So this is what somebody says when they're explaining that they're reading a novel and they know that they're going to be judged harshly for it.' Clearing his throat, he read.

' *"It is only a novel… or, in short, only some work in which the greatest powers of the mind are displayed, in which the most thorough knowledge of human nature, the happiest delineation of its varieties, the liveliest effusions of wit and humour, are conveyed to the world in the best-chosen language."* ' He looked up from the page and caught her eye.

'Jane Austen wrote that?' Melissa said.

'She did indeed. In *Northanger Abbey*.' He showed her the cover. 'It's good, isn't it?'

'Hmmmm,' Melissa said, 'quite good, I suppose.'

Warwick stroked the open page. 'I love how defensive she is about the novel. How she *knows* the skill and perception involved in writing a story because that's often overlooked by readers, isn't it? I mean, I get that all the time. My books are easy to read and therefore people think they're easy to write.'

'Aren't they?'

'They're *fun* to write,' he said, 'but it's still hard work putting one hundred thousand words in the right order and I love how Jane Austen knew that too. Just think how much harder it was for her too with paper and pen. But what I also love about Jane Austen was that she wasn't just writing about the fluff of life.'

'The fluff of life?' Melissa said, an eyebrow raising imperiously again.

Warwick nodded. 'Some people think she was just writing love stories and there's nothing wrong with that, let me tell you, but Austen did more than that. She truly knew her way not only around the human heart but the human mind too.'

'Right,' Melissa said.

'You don't look convinced,' he said.

'You're trying to convince me?' she said. 'Is that what all this is about with the quotation on tap and the pep talk?'

Warwick hoped to goodness that he wasn't blushing. 'Of course not,' he said. 'I just thought you'd appreciate that passage. As a fellow writer.'

Melissa nodded slowly, eyeing him warily before finishing her coffee. It was then that her phone beeped. She looked down at the screen.

'Dame Pamela wants to meet me and I believe she doesn't like to be kept waiting,' she said, standing up.

'Where are you meeting her?' Warwick asked.

'Outside the Orangery shop,' Melissa said, checking her watch with a grimace. 'I feel like I've been summoned.'

Warwick grinned. 'Good luck,' he said, knowing full well what Dame Pamela had in store for the journalist and hoping that she'd fare better than he had.

Katherine's hand hovered lovingly over a hardback book about the history of Chatsworth which would look utterly splendid on one of their coffee tables at Hawk's Hill. But did they really need another book? She thought about the heaps of books that they had yet to sort out and an internal battle raged within her.

'Excuse me, madam. Do you intend to buy that book?'

'Warwick!' Katherine said, spinning around at his voice.

'It's a very nice book,' he said, picking it up and flipping through the pages.

'Don't we have enough books?'

He gave her a quizzical look. 'How can a doctor of English Literature believe she has enough books?'

'I was just thinking of the awful mess at home.'

'Which we shall sort out,' Warwick said calmly. 'Just imagine them all neatly on their shelves. They're going to virtually disappear.'

She shook her head and laughed at him.

'And then you will bemoan the fact that you didn't buy this book,' he said.

'All right. All right! I give in. I'll buy the book. Only, let's get it later. I don't want to cart it all around the gardens,' she said. 'How did you get on with Melissa?'

Warwick's face clouded over. 'To be honest, I don't really know. I'm not entirely sure she's human. I just can't seem to connect with her.'

'Oh, dear,' Katherine said. 'Well, perhaps, the others will do better.'

'Let's hope so,' Warwick said.

CHAPTER 7

Annie Soames had hoped to lose her mother but she wasn't having any luck.

'Anne!' Mrs Soames barked. 'Wait for me and get hold of this bag.'

The tartan bag held a tartan flask from the nineteen-seventies and went everywhere that Mrs Soames did even though Annie had told her that there were cafes and kiosks galore at Chatsworth.

'Harrumph!' Mrs Soames had said. 'You won't find *me* lining the pockets of the duke and duchess when I can take my own cup of tea.'

The worst of it was that Mrs Soames expected Annie to share it with her.

'Wouldn't you like a *fresh* cup of tea, Mother?' Annie asked her. They'd finished the tour of the house and were near one of the cafes. 'We've got those vouchers to spend.'

'No, I wouldn't. Just look at those prices!' Mrs Soames cried, causing several heads to turn. Annie was used to her mother's head-turning capabilities but it never ceased to embarrass her all the same.

'Look! There's Rose and Roberta,' Annie said, catching sight of the sisters who were seated outside the Orangery.

'I'm not spending good money to sit with those two nitwits,' Mrs Soames said, her voice loud and carrying across the short distance between them.

'Well, *I'd* like to join them,' Annie said daringly, her face heating in a ferocious blush at her mother's words.

She turned to join the two ladies but her mother

grabbed her wrist.

'*Mother!*'

Mrs Soames looked shocked at the tone of her daughter's voice and they glared at each other for a dreadful silent-drenched moment.

'How *dare* you shout at me!' Mrs Soames said, her bosom rising in a great fleshy defiance.

'You hurt my wrist!' Annie said, her voice sounding like a child's.

'I did no such thing,' Mrs Soames told her.

'Yes you did. Now,' Annie said, taking a deep breath and trying to remain calm even though everybody was looking at them, 'I'm going to buy a cup of tea and maybe even a slice of cake–'

Mrs Soames tutted in disapproval.

'And then I'm going to join our friends.' Without further discussion, Annie went to join the queue, her heart racing wildly as she watched her mother leave the scene.

'Did you see that?' Katherine said to Warwick. After walking around the Canal where the Emperor Fountain was, they'd somehow found themselves in the Orangery shop where they were being tempted by yet more books.

'See what?' Warwick asked. He was distracted by a display of his own Regency romances which looked splendid next to a selection of Darcyesque novels.

'Annie and Mrs Soames,' Katherine said. 'They seemed to be having an argument.'

'That doesn't surprise me,' Warwick said.

'It looked pretty heated to me,' Katherine said.

Warwick shook his head. 'Poor Annie,' he said, 'I don't know how she puts up with it.'

'She told me that Mrs Soames didn't want her leaving home at all. Annie was still living with her when she was thirty-one. I think Mrs Soames just wanted somebody to complain to on a daily basis.'

'And a free dogsbody,' Warwick said.

'No doubt,' Katherine said with a sigh.

'Hey!' Warwick said. 'Would it be really touristy to have my photo taken next to my books?'

'I think it would be highly unusual of you not to,' she said, taking her camera out of her handbag.

No sooner had Katherine taken the photograph than a lady in her early twenties approached Warwick.

'Excuse me,' she said. 'Are you Lorna Warwick? I mean Warwick Lawton?'

'I answer to both those names,' Warwick said, a smile bisecting his face.

'Oh!' the lady cried. 'Ellie! Come here – it's Lorna Warwick.'

Another young lady who'd been perusing the bookshelves, turned around and screamed.

'Warwick!' Her hand flew to her mouth and she raced across the shop and grabbed Warwick's arm. 'I love you!' she cried. 'Your books – I love your books!'

'I saw him first,' the other lady said.

'I'm Ellie,' the screaming lady said.

'And I'm Mina,' the first lady said.

'Would you sign some books for us?'

'I would be absolutely delighted,' Warwick said.

Katherine caught his eye and motioned outside as a small crowd started to gather around Warwick. He nodded and she headed out into the sunshine, smiling at Annie who had now joined Rose and Roberta, and hoping to high heaven that she didn't bump into Mrs Soames in the garden. She would, no doubt, be in a terrible mood.

'But when isn't she?' Katherine said to herself. She then spotted Robyn heading towards the greenhouses. 'Robyn!' she cried.

Robyn turned and waved and Katherine caught up with her.

'I've lost Warwick to some fans in the shop,' she said.

Robyn laughed. 'He does seem to attract the girls now that his true identity is known.'

'Yes, he really knows how to hold court. Just like Dame Pamela,' Katherine said, 'but I sometimes can't help wishing that we could turn back the clock and not have all this adulation. It would be nice to come somewhere like this and just be an ordinary couple.'

'There's nothing ordinary about you two,' Robyn said. 'You're special.'

Katherine returned her smile. 'You're very sweet,' she said. 'Shall we sit down?'

They found a bench made out of a roughly-hewn piece of wood. It was situated under a fine yew tree above the greenhouses with a spectacular view of the grounds and the neat, tree-dotted landscape beyond.

Robyn opened her handbag and retrieved a rather battered copy of *Pride and Prejudice* – the one featuring Keira Knightley and Matthew Macfadyen on the cover.

'This one seemed most appropriate for today,' she said.

'One of my favourites is the Longman Literature edition,' Katherine said. 'It's got a beautiful blue cover, illustrated with swirling dancers and a lovely Regency lady at its centre.'

'I have that one too,' Robyn said. 'Amongst many

others.'

'Of course,' Katherine said and they laughed. 'So, what did you think of the house?'

'It's left me breathless,' Robyn said. 'I think you could fit fifty Purley Halls into it – at least!'

'Or two hundred Hawk's Hills,' Katherine said.

'It wouldn't suit me,' Robyn admitted. 'I love seeing these places but Horseshoe Cottage is my perfect home. But it was so exciting to see the Painted Hall and to walk in the steps of Elizabeth.' She tapped the photo of Keira Knightley on the cover of her paperback. 'The rest of the rooms in this version were filmed in another house, weren't they?'

'Yes,' Katherine said. 'Wilton House near Salisbury.'

'Perhaps Dame Pamela will arrange a weekend there one day,' Robyn said, gazing out across the immaculate lawns towards the house. 'Do you think Jane Austen had Chatsworth in mind when she wrote Pemberley?' she asked after a moment.

'Well, it's a little ambiguous,' Katherine said. 'It could well be Chatsworth and she mentions it at the beginning of volume three when they first arrive in Derbyshire.'

Robyn nodded and flipped through the pages. 'Here,' she said a second later. 'She writes "all the celebrated beauties of Matlock, Chatsworth, Dovedale or the Peak." '

'That's right,' Katherine said. 'But the date of Pemberley is never given. The Gardiners are speculating about it after the house tour, remember?'

Robyn nodded again. 'I think the word used is "conjecturing".'

Katherine laughed. 'You know the novel better

than I do,' she said. 'Perhaps you should come and take some of my tutorials some time.'

Robyn grinned. 'I'm just a fan – not an academic. I doubt if I could teach anyone anything more than how wonderful Mr Darcy is.' Robyn's eyes scanned the pages again. 'Here's a description,' she said a minute later. ' "It was a large, handsome, stone building, standing well on rising ground." '

'But that could be any date at all,' Katherine said.

'Do you think Pemberley could be older than Chatsworth?'

'I really think it might be. After all, you wouldn't "conjecture" over the date of a contemporary building, would you?'

Robyn looked thoughtful. 'Perhaps it's actually Haddon Hall – that's near Bakewell just as Pemberley was.'

Katherine nodded. 'Yes, it could well be.'

'But that has a far more Brontean feel about it, don't you think? All medieval turrets and castellations.'

'But that's a modern audience's interpretation of it. Jane Austen might have viewed it quite differently and it could still be all elegance inside as Pemberley was described.'

'It's stood in as Thornfield in at least two adaptations of *Jane Eyre*, hasn't it?' Robyn said.

'You're a Bronte fan too?'

'It's hard not to be,' Robyn said, 'although the Brontes come a very poor second to Jane.' She read some more of her book quietly to herself. 'There are woods mentioned and a river and bridge just like here at Chatsworth,' she said a moment later.

'You know, I think there are probably elements of

Chatsworth in there – the interior of Pemberley certainly has the elegance of Chatsworth but lots of writers amalgamate difference places and then throw in a good measure of their own imagination too. I think, for most Austen fans, Chatsworth will always be Pemberley just as Castle Howard will always be Brideshead.'

'You think it foolish to try and find the real Pemberley?' Robyn asked.

'Not foolish, exactly,' Katherine said. 'I think we all carry it inside us, don't we? We each have our own individual version that no film director can ever really create for us.'

Robyn laughed. 'I think it's funny that Elizabeth tells Jane that her feelings for Mr Darcy began when she saw "his beautiful grounds at Pemberley",' she said.

Katherine laughed. 'I know. But don't forget that that's when she learned about his true character from the housekeeper.'

'Of course,' Robyn said. 'Our Elizabeth would never have married simply for a beautiful home – however stunning it might be.'

Robyn's mind drifted, once again, across the miles from Derbyshire to Hampshire and she wished with all her heart that she could glimpse what her beloved Dan was doing at that very moment.

CHAPTER 8

'I can't believe this has happened,' Dan said through gritted teeth. He was sitting in the drawing room at Purley Hall having been fed tea and shortbread by a very sympathetic Higgins.

'Should I ring Miss Robyn?' Higgins asked.

'Good grief no!' Dan said, his bright eyes widening in alarm. 'She mustn't know about this or she'll be on the first train home. I don't want to panic her. She's been looking forward to this weekend for months and I'm not going to wreck it for her.'

'Well, if you're quite sure–'

'I'm sure,' Dan said, shaking his head at the unfortunate predicament he found himself in. Luckily, nothing was broken but Dan had sustained one hefty horse kick to his lower right leg and the bruising was substantial.

'You'll have to keep your weight off that leg,' he'd been told at the hospital and he'd been sent home with a pair of unwieldy crutches and Higgins fussing over him like an old woman.

'Perhaps I can be of assistance with Miss Cassandra,' Higgins said now.

'What?' Dan said, trying to imagine Higgins taking care of a toddler and not able to hold the picture in his mind at all. 'No, no, no. I'll manage,' he said, struggling to his feet. 'You've done so much for me already.'

'If I may be permitted to voice an opinion?' Higgins said.

'Voice away,' Dan said.

'Miss Cassandra is at the running around like a

tornado stage, is she not?'

'Yes,' Dan said, 'she is indeed.'

'I fear it will be difficult to keep up with her whilst on a pair of crutches.'

Dan sighed. 'Difficult but not impossible,' he said.

'And the dogs, sir?'

'I'll cope.'

'And the horses?'

'I've got help with those,' Dan said. 'The girls have texted me and everything's fine. Rosie caught Winter and she's in her stable.' He was beginning to get exasperated by Higgins's lack of faith in him. 'I can cope.'

Higgins nodded. 'Yes, sir,' he said but he didn't look convinced.

Doris Norris was wearing a funny little summer hat in pink and white checks that kept flopping over her left eye. She took it off when she entered the house, squashing it into her handbag and popping a mint humbug into her mouth in order to keep her strength up. She had been going to walk around the house with Rose and Roberta but there had been some confusion when Roberta had disappeared in the kitchen garden and Doris had found herself on her own after Rose had gone in search of her sister. Doris didn't mind, of course. Since her dear husband's death, she'd been used to being on her own.

Still, she couldn't help thinking it would have been nice to have had some company as she walked through the lavish rooms, nodding at the paintings and catching her breath at the views from the windows.

At the end of the tour, she found herself in the

sculpture gallery. It was so bright in there that Doris reached into her bag for her hat and squashed it down onto her head again.

'That's better,' she said.

'Did you say something?' a gentleman with startling white hair said.

'Pardon?' Doris said.

'Did you say something?' the man repeated.

'No,' Doris said, a little perplexed.

The man smiled at her and, pushing her hat out of her eyes again, she smiled back.

'Davey,' he said. 'My name's Davey.'

'Doris,' Doris said, taking a seat in the middle of the room.

The man sat down beside her. 'It's certainly warm, isn't it?'

'A little too warm for me,' Doris confessed.

'An English rose,' he said.

'Pardon?' Doris said, wondering if she'd heard him right and hoping he didn't think she was deaf.

'You have the complexion of an English rose,' he said.

Doris smiled. 'Well, if that means I'm a little pale and apt to wilt then I suppose you're right.'

'My skin's as tough as a rhino hide,' he said and Doris saw that he certainly had a good tanned complexion. 'Spent years out in Kenya.'

'Really?'

He nodded. 'How about you?'

'I've never left the Cotswolds,' Doris said. 'Although I did once go on a package holiday to Gibraltar but I missed the green fields of England. I was only away for a week.'

Davey laughed. 'I missed England too,' he said. 'It

takes some beating, doesn't it?'

'Oh, yes,' Doris said, 'and a day out like today couldn't ever be matched in another country. A fine stately home and a stroll around beautiful gardens followed by a proper cup of tea – that's what makes me happy.'

'Me too,' he said. 'My travelling days are over now.'

They sat in affable silence for a while.

'My Judy used to love it here,' Davey said at last. 'She's why I'm here now.'

'Your wife?'

He nodded. 'She died two years ago.'

'I'm sorry,' Doris said. 'I lost my husband many years ago but I still miss him every day.'

'It doesn't get any easier, does it?' he said, his eyes large and melancholy.

'No,' Doris said. 'It only gets different.'

They looked at each other and exchanged soft smiles.

'How long are you in Derbyshire?' he asked at last.

'Just for the weekend,' Doris told him. 'I'm with a group of Jane Austen fans and we're staying at The Wye Hotel just outside Bakewell.'

'Very nice,' he said.

'I was hoping to see Darcy's bust today,' Doris said.

'Excuse me?' Davey looked startled.

'The bust they had made for the film of *Pride and Prejudice*. I believe they used to have it up in the shop but a young man told me it's been moved into the private part of the house.' She gave a little giggle. 'I expect the duchess has it in her bedroom.'

Davey smiled. 'Just what is it with women and this

Mr Darcy?' he asked.

'Why, he's the ultimate hero,' she said.

'Is he, indeed?'

'Oh, yes,' Doris said.

'And he's why you and your friends are here today?'

'Pretty much,' Doris said, standing up. 'Oh, dear!'

'Are you all right?' Davey asked. He was on his feet in an instant, offering a helping hand.

'I just felt a little dizzy,' Doris said. 'It's this heat. It's all a bit too much for me these days, I'm afraid.'

Davey nodded. 'How about we find some shade and have a nice cup of tea?'

Doris beamed him a smile. 'That sounds absolutely smashing.'

'She has *no* right to talk to you like that,' Roberta was saying to Annie. They'd left the cafe together and were walking towards the Canal and the Emperor Fountain.

'She's my mother. I've come to expect it,' Annie said with a resigned sigh.

Roberta shook her head. 'How awful for you, my dear.' She rested her hand on Annie's arm and Annie felt tears vibrating in her eyes. Blinking them back quickly, she gazed back at the house. She wasn't going to let her mother ruin her day. She'd done that too many times in the past.

'Do you mind if we don't talk about it all?' she said and Roberta nodded.

'Of course I don't mind.'

'Yes,' Rose said, 'we should be talking about Mr Darcy and Elizabeth Bennet.'

Roberta nodded. 'Ah, indeed! How I adore the

scenes at Pemberley,' she said as they began the long walk around the impressive water feature known as the Canal Pond, taking in the great jet of water that thundered up into the air. 'I love seeing Elizabeth's response when she hears all the wonderful things the housekeeper says about her master and the Gardiners are equally baffled because Elizabeth has told them what an awful man he is.'

Rose nodded as they walked along the top of a steep bank whose slopes were covered in wild flowers.

'My favourite bit is when it says that Elizabeth is beginning to think of Mr Darcy with "a more gentle sensation". Isn't that gorgeous?'

Annie joined in. 'I like the bit when their eyes meet and they both blush. That's *so* romantic!'

' "Never had he spoken with such gentleness",' Rose quoted and the two sisters sighed in unison.

'What did you think of the adaptation of *Death Comes to Pemberley*?' Annie asked when they reached the far side of the Canal Pond and stopped to admire the famous view down the long stretch of water back to the house.

'Well, it was beautifully shot,' Rose said, 'but I don't like it when people mess with Jane Austen's characters – they should create their own. After all, the word "novel" means "new", doesn't it?'

'But I did love that scene at the end with Georgiana,' Roberta enthused.

'Well, who wouldn't love a man on horseback riding towards you to sweep you off your feet?' Rose said.

'Indeed, sister. And we got to see Mr Darcy and Elizabeth in bed with each other,' Roberta pointed out.

'Well, really! Trust you to remember that scene.'

'You remember it too,' Roberta chided.

The three of them began the long walk back down the other side of the Canal, passing tourists who were sitting on the grass or having their photos taken.

'I think I'll stop here a while,' Annie said.

Rose and Roberta looked at her.

'Are you sure? We're going to try and find that wonderful water tree. Won't you join us?' Rose asked.

'I'm just going to sit for a bit,' Annie said, a little smile doing its best to light up her pale face.

'Okay, my dear,' Roberta said. 'We'll see you later.'

Annie watched as the two sisters walked away from her. They were such sweethearts but even their delightful chatter hadn't managed to pull her out of her glumness.

She sighed. She should have been thinking of Pemberley and Mr Darcy. She'd been a fan ever since she'd first seen the great hero played by Laurence Olivier. The scene that had done it for her had been when he'd been teaching Greer Garson's Elizabeth archery and had placed his arms around her body in order to do so. It was a scene which was not to be found in Jane Austen's masterpiece but it was, nevertheless, a most welcome one. But Annie Soames wasn't thinking the thoughts of a Janeite as she sat on the grass near the Emperor Fountain; she was thinking about the horrible humiliation she had suffered – yet again – at the hands of her mother.

Craning her neck back and closing her eyes against the brilliance of the sunshine, she wondered why she still put up with it. Her mother would never change, would she? The long years of being bossed around had taught Annie that and yet she'd so hoped that this little break would be different – that the delight of a whole weekend talking about Jane Austen and being in the company of fellow Janeites would ease things between her and her mother. But, from what Annie had deduced from the new friends she had made on the trip so far, her mother's foul moods and bossy ways didn't even abate for Austen.

'Well, I don't like to speak ill of anybody,' Doris Norris had said to Annie just the night before after Annie had asked what her mother was like during the Jane Austen weekends at Purley, 'but your mother can be – how shall I put it? Difficult?'

Annie gave a hollow laugh. *Difficult!* That was putting it mildly.

She thought back to the many many difficult situations her mother had created for her like the time at primary school when Annie had volunteered to take care of the school rabbits during the summer holidays.

'You're not bringing those home,' Mrs Soames had said at the top of her voice in front of everybody at the school gate. 'Filthy, dirty creatures.'

Then there had been the time at middle school when she'd brought Christopher round for tea. She'd had a bit of a crush on him and couldn't believe he had said yes to her invitation. And what had her mother gone and said? Annie remembered it as if it was yesterday.

'You didn't pick your knickers up off the bedroom floor this morning, Anne! *I* had to do it,' she'd said, causing both Annie and Christopher to blush intensely. Of course, it hadn't stopped there; a fierce whispering campaign went on at school after the knickers-on-the-floor incident much to Annie's mortification. Indeed, it still made her shudder now when she thought about it. Such childhood scars never really healed, did they?

If only her mother could relax, Annie thought, but she was as tightly wound up as ever even at a place like Chatsworth. Annie had sincerely thought that the magic of being at a real life Pemberley would have gone some way to making her mother smile but it obviously wasn't going to happen and she had to admit defeat.

She tried to empty her mind of all thoughts of her mother and focus on the soothing sounds around her. How wonderfully refreshing was the sound of running water around the Chatsworth estate on that hot July day, Annie thought, from the delicate trickle of water from the willow tree fountain to the tremendous splash of the Emperor Fountain which now filled her ears, lulling her into a blissful half-slumber.

But it wasn't to last.

'ANNE!'

The voice that assaulted her ears could only belong to one person.

'Where have you been all this time?' The bulk of her mother's figure hovered menacingly between her and the sunshine, instantly blocking its warmth.

Annie opened her eyes and sighed as she greeted her mother's displeased expression.

CHAPTER 9

Katherine and Robyn had left the little bench under the yew tree and were walking around the kitchen garden.

'I hope Dan's remembered to feed the hens,' Robyn said, spying some huge cabbages.

'I'm sure he has,' Katherine said.

'And Cassie!'

Katherine laughed. 'He wouldn't forget to feed his daughter, would he?'

Robyn smiled. 'I'm sure he wouldn't.' A tiny frown wrinkled her brow as she pushed her corkscrew curls away from her face. 'No! I'm *absolutely* sure he wouldn't.' She laughed.

'You hate being away from him, don't you?' Katherine said.

Robyn nodded as she stopped to admire some ruby-bright redcurrants. 'I can't imagine life without him now,' she said.

'I know what you mean,' Katherine said. 'I feel that way about Warwick. Crazy, eh? I used to be convinced I was going to spend my life on my own, my head buried in my books and papers and maybe occasionally getting my hopes up and going on yet another horrendous date. Then Warwick ran over my foot with his suitcase, told me a lot of ridiculous lies about who he was and made me fall madly in love with him.'

'I often wonder what would have happened if I hadn't gone to Purley Hall that autumn, don't you?'

Katherine gave a little shiver. 'I can't imagine,' she said.

'It might not have been any different for you, though,' Robyn said. 'I mean, you were already friends with Warwick, weren't you?'

Katherine nodded. 'Yes.'

'I bet you would have met up sooner or later,' Robyn said.

'You're probably right.'

They exchanged smiles and continued walking.

'Robyn,' Katherine said after a moment's pause. 'Do you mind if I ask you something?'

Robyn looked at her friend. 'Ask away.'

Katherine cleared her throat.

'What is it?' Robyn prompted her. They'd climbed to the top of the garden and found a bright blue bench to sit on.

'How did you know you were ready to start a family?' Katherine asked at last.

Robyn blinked in surprise at the question. She really hadn't been expecting that.

'Well,' she said, 'it happened rather quickly for us. I'd just moved into Horseshoe Cottage. It kind of took us by surprise although we were both delighted. We didn't tell anyone until after the wedding but I'm sure Pammy had guessed.'

'But you would have got married anyway, wouldn't you?'

'Of course,' Robyn said. 'I feel as if my whole life has been leading up to this moment now – this wonderful life with Dan and Cassie and my work at Purley. I sometimes think I'm the luckiest girl in the world.'

Katherine smiled. 'You deserve it after all you've been through.'

Robyn's eyes shone brightly as she gazed down

upon the garden. 'I've *always* known I wanted children – with the right man, of course,' she said.

Katherine nodded. 'Yes, that plays a big part.'

'And I'll tell you a little secret,' she said. 'I'm absolutely ready for another child.'

'Oh, Robyn! How lovely.'

'Horseshoe Cottage will be getting a little cramped soon.'

'You might have to move into Purley Hall,' Katherine said.

'Oh, no,' Robyn said. 'I wouldn't leave our cottage for anything. We'll manage, I'm sure.'

They got up and walked slowly through a wooded section of the grounds until they found themselves at the top of the cascade.

'Do you think you're ready then?' Robyn asked. 'I mean, to start a family.'

Katherine looked down the hill at the fabulous water feature, watching as a little boy of about seven paddled on one of the steps, his hands held tightly by his father.

'I'm not sure,' Katherine said. 'Warwick is, though. He's more than ready. I think he'd fill the whole of Hawk's Hill in record time if he could but–'

'But?'

'It's never crossed my mind before. I mean, not seriously,' Katherine said. 'I'm not used to being married and living with someone. I think I've still got this spinster career woman mindset or something.' She gave a little laugh.

'But life doesn't always turn out the way you think it will,' Robyn said, 'and that can be rather wonderful.'

'I know,' Katherine said, 'but I'm so used to

being in charge of everything. I like organisation and planning things and I never planned for any of this to happen. It always happened to other people or to the people I read about in Jane Austen and Warwick's Lorna books. I really never thought this would be on the agenda.'

Robyn bit her lip. 'But there's no rush, is there?'

'Well, I'm not getting any younger!'

'Oh, rubbish! You've got lots of child-bearing years in you,' Robyn said with a little laugh.

Katherine's eyes widened. 'Now, that sounds absolutely terrifying!'

Robyn shook her head. 'But it isn't really,' she said. 'You just take it one wonderful moment at a time.'

Katherine looked at Robyn. 'You are such a romantic,' she said.

'I know!' Robyn said. 'I can't help it. Life is full of these amazing moments now I've got Dan and I sometimes have to stop – put down whatever I'm doing – and enjoy it all.' She reached a hand out and placed it on Katherine's arm. 'Don't think too much about these things,' she said. 'Just let them happen.'

'I'm afraid I always think everything through *very* thoroughly,' Katherine admitted with a sigh.

'Well, it's good to be organised but not everything in life *can* be organised,' Robyn said. 'Life with Dan and Cassie and the animals has taught me that. You've got to let go and respond to things as they happen sometimes. It's often more fun that way.'

Katherine nodded as they walked down the long slope back towards the house. 'I know you're right,' she said, 'and I don't know why I worry all the time.'

'No, you should relax, lay back and think of Mr

Darcy!' Robyn said and they both laughed.

Dame Pamela was holding court with Melissa Berry. At least, that's what it seemed like to the young journalist. She'd heard the great actress recount several of her most famous performances before she'd launched into what seemed like a lecture about the glories of Jane Austen.

'You mustn't try to rush through her prose,' Dame Pamela was saying. 'It should be savoured like a fine wine. Her wit, her elegance of expression, her–'

'But I really prefer modern fiction,' Melissa interrupted. Dame Pamela did *not* appreciate being interrupted. She twisted one of her diamond rings, cleared her throat in consternation and began again.

'But who do you think modern writers have to thank if not Jane Austen? She was ground-breaking – the first real chick lit author and that's a term I don't like to use but it's what all you young ones are familiar with, isn't it? Well, our Jane was the first to write the modern romance – the classic boy meets girl book.'

'I suppose,' Melissa said, stifling a yawn.

Dame Pamela flinched. She had never *ever* – at least to her knowledge – made anybody yawn before. This young woman really was the limit.

'Anyway,' Dame Pamela said, getting up from her chair with a noisy, displeased scrape, 'you would do well to persevere with Jane Austen for there is no finer literature in the English language.'

Melissa Berry opened her handbag and got her mobile out and Dame Pamela felt the spirit of Lady Catherine de Bourgh rise inside her – the scene where she is shocked and displeased by the outspoken Elizabeth Bennet. Dame Pamela was on the verge of announcing that she was "most seriously displeased" but knew that the reference would fall flat on the journalist. Instead, she levelled the sort of glare that was enough to have a grown man shaking in his shoes – all except Higgins, that was, because he was used to his mistress' death glares. But Melissa was totally oblivious because she was busy texting.

At Horseshoe Cottage in Hampshire, Dan Harcourt had managed to crash into a side table and knock a lamp onto the floor, had become entangled with a pile of washing he'd left in the kitchen and had walloped poor Biscuit with the end of his right crutch. The little terrier had yelped and retreated to his basket by the Aga, an accusatory look on his furry little face. Life on crutches, Dan had to admit, wasn't as easy as he'd first thought.

But he soldiered on, hobbling to the stables to check everything was running smoothly and to be there in time for Jack who was arriving for his lesson on Gemini.

'Been in the wars?' Jack asked as he arrived ten minutes later.

'Don't ask,' Dan said. There was no way he was going to admit to Jack that his injury was inflicted by a horse – not just as his student's confidence was building.

The lesson went well, with Jack really beginning to look like "a hero on horseback" which had been his goal when he'd first signed up for lessons.

'Well done, mate,' Dan said as Jack left the stables after his lesson. 'We're nearly there.'

After struggling on his own to untack, groom and turn out Gemini, Dan hobbled back to Horseshoe

Cottage, leaving the rest of the horses in the capable hands of the girls he employed. He had a couple of hours before Cassie was due back and he planned on doing nothing more than feeding the hens some corn and letting the dogs out in the garden whilst sitting in a deckchair with a glass of something tall and cool. But that wasn't to be for, when he opened the front door, the sound of something exploding met his ears.

CHAPTER 10

'I've been looking high and low for you,' Mrs Soames said, glaring down at her daughter. 'Fancy storming off like that!'

'But I didn't storm off,' Annie said, feeling dazed from having nodded off in the sunshine. 'It was *you* who did the storming.'

Mrs Soames tutted. 'Ridiculous child!'

Annie sighed as she got up. How many times had she told her mother that she wasn't a child? She'd lost count and it didn't matter really because she'd still be treated like one.

'What have you been doing, anyway?' Mrs Soames asked her daughter.

'Just sitting,' she said. How did her mother make everything sound like an accusation? It really was a special gift she had.

'Come on. I want my picture taken by the fountain.'

Having just walked through Paxton's rock garden, Katherine and Robyn were heading towards the Emperor Fountain. Katherine had rung her errant husband on his mobile and the two had arranged to meet there.

'I want to see the shot that's in the film,' Robyn said. 'You know when Elizabeth arrives in the carriage with the Gardiners?'

'We'll have to walk to the other end of the Canal Pond for that,' Katherine told her as she studied the map. 'Oh, look. There's Warwick!'

Katherine and Robyn waved.

'He's found Dame Pamela,' Robyn said. 'I wonder how she got on with Melissa.'

They didn't have to wait long to find out.

'I have never ever been *so* frustrated by anyone in my life,' Dame Pamela said, casting her eyes to the blue sky above. 'Other than myself, of course, when I broke a leg and had to pull out of Ibsen's *The Doll's House* at The Old Vic.'

Robyn grinned. She loved these little glimpses into Dame Pamela's illustrious past.

'She'll come round,' Robyn said.

'You really believe that?' Dame Pamela said. 'Warwick didn't get anywhere with her either and now she's gone flouncing off towards the greenhouses.'

'Oh, dear,' Robyn said. 'Well, maybe our film evening will help sway her.'

'If you ask me, it's all a terrible waste of time,' Dame Pamela said.

'Don't give up, Pammy!' Robyn said, resting a hand on her shoulder and getting a handful of shoulder-pad instead.

Dame Pamela turned and gave her young sister-in-law a smile. 'Sweet girl,' she said.

'Oh, my God!' Warwick suddenly cried. 'Poor Annie.'

They all looked in the direction Warwick was nodding in to see Mrs Soames flinging her handbag at Annie and waving her arms in the air in bossy direction.

'Shall we go and rescue her?' Katherine said and the four of them headed across the grass towards the Emperor Fountain where Annie was doing her best to photograph her mother.

'Don't stick your finger over the camera,' Mrs

Soames said.

'I'm not going to stick my finger over the camera,' Annie said.

'I haven't paid all this money to have a photo of your finger.'

Katherine, Warwick, Robyn and Dame Pamela watched as Annie took a succession of photos on the instruction of Mrs Soames.

'Portrait, Anne, *not* landscape! And make sure you've got the fountain in it.'

'Hi, Annie,' Robyn called. 'Would you like me to take one of you both together?'

'No,' Mrs Soames said. 'Just me. Move a bit closer this time.'

The group watched as Mrs Soames manoeuvred herself a little closer to the water feature.

'Not too close, Mother,' Annie warned.

'I'm not going to be silly enough to fall in,' Mrs Soames said and she didn't but what did catch her unawares was a freak gust of wind which caught the great spray of water from the Emperor Fountain and sent it in her direction.

Mrs Soames cried in alarm as the freezing water soaked into the material of her skirt, revealing rather more curves than anybody ever wanted to see. Warwick guffawed and immediately got an elbow in his ribs from Katherine and Dame Pamela bit her lip in an attempt not to laugh.

'Oh, Mrs Soames! Are you all right?' Robyn asked, running forward.

'Do I *look* all right?' Mrs Soames barked, pulling at her skirt.

'Well, no,' Robyn admitted. 'You look rather wet.'

'Stupid girl – *do* something!'

Robyn rooted around in the large canvas bag she was carrying full of emergency supplies like sun cream and plasters just in case any Janeites came a cropper at Chatsworth.

'Here,' she said a moment later, handing a long cotton scarf in shades of pink, blue and silver to Mrs Soames.

'What am I meant to do with *that*?' the cantankerous old woman barked.

'Erm – how about tying it around your waist to cover your – erm – bottom,' Robyn said hesitantly.

It was more than Warwick could bear and he burst out laughing, his eyes streaming with tears of sheer glee. Mrs Soames glared at him before covering her sopping derriere with Robyn's rather insubstantial scarf.

'Let's get you to the ladies',' Robyn said. 'See if we can fix things under a hand dryer.'

Again, Warwick's laughter spilled over, causing him to receive another shove in the ribs from Katherine.

'Warwick!' she hissed as Mrs Soames was led away by Robyn, with Annie in reluctant attendance.

'I can't help it, he said.

Dame Pamela had started chuckling too and the sight of the great actress's shoulders jigging in mirth set Katherine off. The three of them made quite a sight, standing there by the Emperor Fountain, tears rolling down their faces in torrents not dissimilar to the great plume of water.

Doris Norris felt greatly revived after a cup of tea and a slice of cake and was now making her way towards the shady part of the garden where the willow tree fountain was. Davey was with her. In fact, the two of them hadn't stopped talking since they'd met in the sculpture gallery. It was quite extraordinary how well they got on. They both loved gardening, theatre, cooking and literature although Davey had to admit to never having read a Jane Austen novel but Doris forgave him this one little sin. Nobody was perfect, after all.

Reaching, the fountain, they stood and gazed at it in its shady setting.

'Wonderfully cool here,' Doris said.

'You're feeling better now?' Davey asked.

'Much, thank you.' She was still wearing her funny little hat and had just applied some more sun cream. 'What?'

'You have some – erm'

'Have some what?'

Davey smiled and took a step forward, his index finger reaching out to smooth a little blob of sun cream on the end of Doris's nose.

'Oh!' she cried out. 'How embarrassing.'

'It looked like a little snowflake,' Davey said, giving her another of his smiles which reminded Doris of Crispin Bonham-Carter's Mr Bingley in the 1995 adaptation of *Pride and Prejudice* and that meant it was very cute indeed.

They walked around the willow tree fountain with Davey offering a supporting arm for Doris to link hers in as it was quite slippery but wonderfully refreshing to be so close to the water on such a hot day.

'Isn't it pretty?' she said. 'I wonder if I could fit one in my garden.

They talked again about their respective gardens.

Davey was very much a lawn man – taking great care in maintaining an immaculate sward – but he was also a passionate plantsman and what he didn't know about irises really wasn't worth knowing at all.

'You know, I haven't talked to a woman like this for ages,' Davey said and then chuckled. 'Well, I haven't talked like this to *anyone*, if I'm honest. You're a very easy woman to talk to, Doris.'

'Well, you're very easy to listen to,' she said as they left the willow tree fountain and walked out into the sunshine by the cascade.

He took a deep breath. 'Can I ask you something?'

'Of course.'

'This isn't being too forward I hope,' he said.

'What isn't?' Doris asked.

'I should very much like to see you again,' he said.

'Oh,' Doris said.

'Would that be okay?' he asked, his head cocked to one side. 'I mean, say no if I'm boring you and you never want to clap eyes on me again.'

'You're not boring me,' Doris said. 'Quite the opposite, in fact.'

'Really?'

She nodded, her pink and white checked hat flopping over her eyes. 'And I should very much like to see you again.'

Looking absolutely chuffed, Davey offered Doris his arm again and it was then that something occurred to her.

The bouquet. I caught the bouquet at Katherine and Warwick's wedding, Doris thought, a tiny blush colouring her cheeks.

The day at Chatsworth drew to a close all too quickly

for the Purley Hall holidaymakers and there were more than a few red shoulders and happy faces when they all met up in the car park at closing time. Mrs Soames was uncharacteristically quiet on the minibus back to the hotel in Bakewell and nobody dared to breathe a word about the whole watery business until she had shuffled off to her room and they were safely out of earshot in the hotel bar.

'Oh, I *was* sorry to have missed the fun,' Roberta said.

Rose tutted and Doris Norris giggled.

'I should like to have seen it too,' Doris admitted. 'I could have Tweeted it with my new phone.'

'You have a Twitter account?' Robyn said, impressed.

Doris Norris nodded. 'Of course,' she said. 'My grandson set it up for me. "At Doris Norris" I believe it is.'

Robyn grinned. Wonders would never cease, she thought.

'Serves the old bag right!' Roberta said.

'Roberta!' her sister admonished.

'Well, she makes everyone's lives a misery especially that poor daughter of hers.'

'And where did you get to all day?' Rose asked Doris.

Doris gave a mischievous little smile. 'I met somebody,' she said.

'Who?' Rose, Roberta and Robyn said in unison.

'A man,' Doris said with a smile before turning and leaving the bar for her room.

'I guess we'll have to see if she Tweets about him,' Roberta said.

'But you're not on Twitter, my dear,' Rose said.

'Am I not? I thought I was.'

'No, that's Facebook,' Rose explained patiently.

'You two are on Facebook?' Robyn said.

'Of course,' Roberta said. 'It's where all the cool people hang out.'

Robyn laughed. 'Listen,' she said, getting back into courier mode, 'we'd better all freshen up and prepare for dinner.'

'And it's the Joe Wright film version tonight, isn't it?' Rose asked.

'Yes,' Robyn said. 'We'll be able to spot all the locations we saw today.' She watched as the two sisters went upstairs to their rooms and then reached for her phone. She was desperate to speak to Dan.

At Horseshoe Cottage, Dan was still recovering from the incident that had occurred earlier. The washing machine door seemed to have exploded and the contents – clothes and water – had spewed out all across the utility room.

Dan had skidded upon entering and had only just retained his balance on his crutches. He was getting things sorted out when there was a knock at the front door. It was the childminder with Cassie who was crying.

'I'm afraid she scraped her knee,' Stacey explained as she walked Cassie into the hall. 'I did tell her not to run after the cat but she wouldn't listen and I couldn't get to her in time because I was feeding baby Joe. I'm so sorry.'

'It's okay,' Dan said. 'She's just like her mum – always wanting to pick up any old animal that crosses her path.'

'And how's life on the crutches?' Stacey asked,

having received a call from Dan about his accident.

'I'm getting there,' he said.

'Well, I'll pick Cassie up again tomorrow morning but do let me know if you need any help in the meantime.'

Dan thanked her and closed the front door. Leaning his crutches against the hallway wall, he scooped Cassie up in his arms.

'What happened to you, my poppet?'

Her bright eyes, that were so like Robyn's, looked up at him full of tears.

'I think an early night for you as soon as you've had some tea.'

She shook her head. 'Hens!' she cried.

Dan sighed and decided to give in because he knew he wouldn't hear the end of it if he didn't.

'Just a quick goodnight as I feed them their corn, then,' he said with a chuckle. She really was *so* like her mother.

At the Wye Hotel, Robyn was wondering why Dan wasn't answering his phone. She looked at her watch. He'd definitely be at home now, she thought. He'd need to be there for Stacey to drop Cassie off. Unless he'd gone up to the stables with their daughter. Cassie was horse mad already and Dan would often take her up in the evenings. She tried his mobile.

'Dan?' she said a moment later.

'Hey, Robyn!'

'Are you at the stables? You didn't pick up the house phone.'

'No. I was in the garden with Cassie. Just got back inside.'

'How is she?'

'She's fine,' he said.

'Yeah?' Robyn said. 'And you? You sound out of breath.'

'I'm fine too,' he said.

'Are you sure?

'Of course I'm sure.'

'How are the dogs and the hens? And the horses?' she added, knowing how much Dan doted on his charges.

'*Everyone's* fine,' he told her again. 'Tell me about your day.'

So she did, recounting the memorable trip to Chatsworth and the incident with Mrs Soames and the Emperor Fountain.

'Now that's a sight I'm glad I missed out on,' Dan said.

'You should have seen her in the ladies with her bottom under the hand dryer. You would have been so proud of me – I didn't laugh once! I was the consummate professional.'

He laughed. 'You were made for that job,' he said. 'You're so good with people.'

Robyn sighed. 'But you and Cassie are the people I really want to be with.'

'And you will be – really soon,' he said.

'I miss you both so much.'

'Nonsense!' he said. 'I bet you didn't think of us *once* as you were walking around the grounds of Mr Darcy's house.'

'That's not true!' Robyn protested.

Dan laughed. 'We miss you,' he said.

'Don't say that or I'll catch the first train back home.'

'No, no,' he said. 'Stay and enjoy every minute and

we'll be waiting here for you when you come home.'

She smiled. 'Love you,' she said.

'Love you too.'

Robyn put her phone down, her eyes misty with happy tears and then she took a deep breath because she had a fun-packed evening to prepare for.

CHAPTER 11

That evening, once everybody had rested and dined, Robyn fixed the chairs so that everybody had a good view of the TV screen and the 2005 film adaptation of *Pride and Prejudice* was shown. Melissa Berry was there, under sufferance, and looked totally bored by the whole thing.

'She's fiddling with her phone,' Doris Norris whispered to Roberta. Dame Pamela turned around in horror and glared at the offending instrument. Melissa Berry looked up and caught the great lady's eye.

'I've just got to reply to this text,' she said.

Dame Pamela cleared her throat and, with a groan, Melissa put her phone away.

'Make sure it's on silent,' Mrs Soames barked.

Melissa took it out of her bag again and switched it off, mouthing the word, 'Satisfied?' to the back of Mrs Soames's head.

'Here it comes!' Rose announced as Elizabeth and the Gardiners set off for Pemberley.

'It's the view from the end of the Canal,' Roberta said as Keira Knightley stood up in the carriage and laughed.

'Oh, I didn't walk that far,' Doris said.

'And there's the Emperor Fountain,' Annie said.

'We all know what happened there,' Roberta said in a none-too-quiet whisper. Warwick immediately guffawed and Dame Pamela let fly a funny little squeal. Mrs Soames shifted uneasily in her chair but remained silent.

As they approached the scene where Elizabeth meets Mr Darcy in the misty morning meadow, the whole room seemed to be holding its breath. Robyn looked across the room towards Melissa and noticed that even she seemed to be spellbound by the scene and that her eyes were glittering with tears. Robyn frowned. Had she got that right? Were they really tears or was it just the reflection of the television screen?

Robyn had her answer a moment later when Melissa got up and hurried out of the room and she didn't need to think twice before following her.

'Melissa?' Robyn cried after her, catching up with her at the foot of the stairs. 'Are you okay?'

Melissa turned her head away so that Robyn couldn't see her face and sniffed loudly.

'I'm fine,' she said unconvincingly.

'You don't look or sound fine,' Robyn said gently.

'It's just hay fever, okay?'

Robyn blinked in surprise at the blatant lie. 'Why don't I get us a couple of drinks and find somewhere quiet to sit?'

Melissa shook her head. 'I'm going up to my room.'

'Oh,' Robyn said.

Melissa started up the stairs.

'Are you sure you don't want to stay? We're going to watch some clips from the BBC version of *Pride and Prejudice* in preparation for our trip to Lyme Park tomorrow. I think you'd enjoy it.'

Melissa shook her head. 'No,' she said. 'I couldn't.'

Robyn frowned as she watched the retreating back of Melissa. She was the most uncommunicative person Robyn had ever met but she couldn't help wanting to talk to her all the same. Something was *obviously* upsetting her.

The next morning, after a hearty breakfast during which Doris Norris had sustained a ten-minute bout of hiccups much to the chagrin of Mrs Soames, who said that Doris had been eating far too many Bakewell puddings for one small person, the minibus left the hotel, crossing the border from Derbyshire into Cheshire.

'Now, I hope you won't be too disappointed to find out that the model of Mr Darcy that was in the lake in front of the house is no longer there,' Dame Pamela announced as they arrived at Lyme Park.

A few of the company groaned.

'Where's it gone?' Roberta asked.

'I believe it was sent to Australia,' Dame Pamela said.

'Darcy down under?' Annie said.

'I would have paid good money to have him in my garden pond,' Doris said. 'Just imagine what the neighbours would say.'

Ten minutes later, they arrived at the house via a shuttle bus, which saved walking up the steep steps from the car park, and they made their way together towards the entrance, entering a courtyard that the eager Janeites recognised instantly.

'Those are the steps Mr Darcy ran down in the adaptation when he was trying to stop Elizabeth from leaving,' Rose said, pointing.

'Yes but did he come down the left-hand side or the right?' Roberta asked as they made their way towards them. These things were of great importance to an Austen fan.

'The left, I think,' Rose said.

The group entered the house and walked around in awed silence.

'It's such a dark interior, isn't it?' Dame Pamela said after a few minutes.

'All that Elizabethan wainscotting,' Annie said. 'I'm not sure I like it.'

'You can see why they filmed the interiors elsewhere,' Robyn said. 'It may look the part of Pemberley from the outside but the interior is so much older. What do you think of it, Melissa?'

'Well, it's not quite to my taste but I can see its appeal.'

Robyn nodded, thinking that Melissa was in a better mood this morning and wondering if she'd written any more about them all yet.

After the tour, the group entered the gift shop which was full of Mr Darcy items that were irresistible to them.

'It's Mr Darcy that sells,' the man behind the till said as Doris Norris approached with a handful of books and postcards. 'We've tried some other books but everybody wants Darcy. Even those postcards of Elizabeth Bennet weren't popular enough to continue stocking.'

Doris Norris smiled. 'Mr Darcy is a one off, isn't he?'

'He certainly is,' the man said. 'Keeps us busy in here, that's for sure.'

Roberta joined Doris at the till and paid for her 'I heart Mr Darcy' bookmark. She only had five similar ones at home which, as any voracious reader knows, is nowhere near enough.

The group split up as they left the house and entered

the gardens. Katherine took Warwick's hand and led him back towards the car park.

'Where are we going?' he asked. 'I thought you wanted to see the gardens and then have lunch with everyone.'

'I do but I want to see something first.'

They walked through the car park and along a track which took them through a gate and out onto the moorland where sheep were grazing. It was nice to get away from the weekend crowds and to breathe in some real country air.

'It says it's a fifteen minute walk,' Katherine said, looking at the guide they'd been given.

'To where?' Warwick asked.

'All will be revealed,' she said. 'We might even get the place to ourselves.'

'Unless Mrs Soames decides to stomp after us.'

'Don't even joke about it,' Katherine said. 'God, that woman! Have you heard the way she speaks to her daughter?'

'Frequently.'

'I don't know how Annie puts up with it.'

'No,' Warwick said. 'She's a sweet soul, isn't she?'

'Mrs Soames told her to put something back in the shop and that she couldn't possibly need any more Darcy trinkets. It was so humiliating for her.'

'I wonder why she came away with her mother if she knew what a nightmare it would be.'

'I guess she's a pretty big Janeite to be willing to put up with Mrs Soames for twenty-four hours a day.'

They strode across the field, the summer wind in their hair.

'I feel like Elizabeth Bennet,' Katherine said.

Warwick grabbed her around her waist. 'So you

do,' he said with a laugh.

'Warwick!' she cried, laughing at his boldness as he kissed her.

'There's only the sheep to spy on us up here,' he said.

'What on *earth* do you mean?' she said, knowing *exactly* what he meant.

'Let me kiss you again,' he whispered in her ear.

She batted him away playfully. 'Come on,' she said. 'I think it's just over here.'

'Spoil sport!' Warwick shouted after her as she took off up the track.

'Hurry up!' she cried, turning back to look at him. 'It's here.'

'*What's* here? What's this all about?'

'Just come and see. *Quickly!*'

'Wow!' he said a moment later and Katherine laughed because they'd found a little piece of landscape that was oh-so-familiar to them.

Rose, Roberta and Doris were taking a slow stroll down to the Dutch garden which was reached by a long slope away from the house.

'It's a proper sunken garden, isn't it?' Rose said.

'This is where Elizabeth walked with the Gardiners in the adaptation,' Roberta said as they saw the intricately laid out garden complete with statues, urns and a pond with a water feature in the middle.

'Oh, dear,' Doris said a moment later. 'It's roped off. I so wanted to walk where Jennifer Ehle had walked.'

Rose nodded, knowing how important these things were to fans.

'It's like the time I went to Florence,' Roberta said.

'I was going to find the spot in that loggia where Helena Bonham Carter's Lucy Honeychurch sat in the film version of *A Room with a View* but it was completely covered in scaffolding. I couldn't get near it.'

'What a shame,' Doris said. 'What did you do?'

'Oh, I went and had the biggest pizza known to mankind and bought a nice leather handbag,' Roberta said with a chuckle.

Robyn was standing on the lawn in front of the house. She'd been hoping to talk to Melissa but had lost her in the excitement of the shop and hadn't seen her since. The gardens at Lyme Park were extensive and it was going to be tricky finding her if she didn't want to be found.

It was as she was walking up the path which Mr Darcy and Elizabeth had walked along in the BBC adaptation that she saw her.

'Melissa!' she called. The young woman turned around, a resigned look on her face at having being discovered. 'I've been looking for you.'

'Why?' Melissa asked as Robyn approached her.

'I was worried about you after last night. Is everything okay?'

'Why shouldn't it be?'

Robyn shrugged. 'Because you look permanently distracted and teary and can't leave your phone alone for more than ten minutes.'

Melissa started walking away. 'It's none of your business.'

'I know,' Robyn said, 'but I can't help feeling a bit responsible for the welfare of everyone on this trip and I don't like seeing anybody sad.'

'You should become a journalist,' Melissa said.

Robyn frowned. 'Me? Why?'

'Because you like stories and you never give up.'

Robyn laughed. 'I can't imagine me doing your job. You've got to be pretty thick-skinned, haven't you?'

'I suppose,' Melissa said. 'There are a lot of knock-backs.'

Robyn nodded. 'Is that what's getting you down at the moment? Work?'

They walked along a path that skirted an immaculate lawn.

'It isn't work,' Melissa said. 'I love my job.'

'Personal then?'

'Yes,' Melissa snapped but then she stopped walking and turned to face Robyn. A strange moment passed between them in which neither of them spoke. They seemed to be simply moving towards each other, gauging one another.

'Look,' Robyn said gently, 'I'm a pretty good listener. Why don't you tell me what's going on?'

CHAPTER 12

High above Lyme Park in Drinkwater Meadow, Katherine and Warwick stood spell bound as they gazed at the little lake.

'So, this is where the immortal scene happened,' Katherine said, thinking of the genius moment created by the pen of Andrew Davies when Mr Darcy had removed his dark jacket, cravat, waistcoat, breeches and boots before diving into the lake on that hot summer's day. 'Tempted?' She turned dark, sparkling eyes to her husband.

'It's certainly warm enough,' Warwick said.

Katherine's smile spread over her face. 'Go on,' she said.

Warwick's eyebrows rose a fraction. 'You wouldn't let me give you a little kiss and cuddle but you want me to strip off and dive into the lake?'

'You mean you wouldn't if I asked you *really* nicely?' she asked batting her eyelashes in an over-exaggerated manner.

Warwick laughed. 'Have I ever refused you anything?' he said.

'Yes!' she countered.

'Like what?'

'You never let me see your manuscripts when you're working on them.' Her hands were on her hips now and her brow was furrowed.

'That's because I'm protecting your enjoyment as a reader,' he said.

'Rubbish!' she cried. 'You don't want me reading them in case I interfere with them.'

'Well, there's that too,' he said. 'I don't want your

doctor of literature's nose poking into my stories.'

Katherine smiled. 'Quite right too,' she said. 'Although I wouldn't *dream* of interfering.'

Warwick gave her a quizzical look. 'Really?'

'Of course I wouldn't! Well, unless I saw an absolutely massive hole in your plot.'

'There are no holes in my plots,' Warwick said, taking a step towards her and kissing the tip of her nose.

'I know,' Katherine said, 'I also know that you're trying to distract me with all this in the hope that I'll forget about your swim in the lake.'

Warwick's mouth dropped open in surprise. 'I am not!' he said indignantly.

'No?'

'No!'

Slowly, his fingers began to undo the buttons on his white shirt, revealing a tanned chest but he was only half-way done when a group of hikers appeared from over the hill and he hurriedly did them all back up again.

Katherine giggled and the two of them set off across the meadow back to Lyme Park.

Robyn and Melissa were sitting on a bench in the garden. They'd been there for a good five minutes without speaking and Robyn was beginning to get nervous. This wasn't going to work, was it? Who was she to think that Melissa would just open up to her? It was foolish of her even to attempt to try and understand and help her. Dan was always telling her that she should stop worrying about other people.

'You're too kind-hearted, Robyn,' he'd tell her. 'You always end up hurting yourself when you can't help others.'

She thought back to the incident Dan was referring to when Robyn had tried to help Mr Cuthbert in the village. He was a renowned miserly misery and nobody had anything to do with him but Robyn was quite determined to make him a part of village life. Until he'd thrown that ashtray at her and told her to bugger off and mind her own business, that was.

Robyn shook her head as she remembered the scene. Yet here she was again, quite determined to stick her nose into somebody else's business and try to help them. She took a deep breath. She'd silently count to ten and, if Melissa hadn't said anything to her by then, Robyn would walk away.

One. Two. Three. Four. Fi—

'My fiancé left me,' Melissa suddenly said.

Robyn gasped. 'He did?'

Melissa nodded, her eyes bright with tears. 'That's why I'm here this weekend. My boss asked if there was anyone who wanted to cover this story and I just had to get away so I lied and said I was this big Jane Austen fan.'

'Well, maybe you will be after this weekend,' Robyn said gently.

'Everybody keeps cornering me, trying to tell me what a great writer she is when all I want to do is tell them that anybody who writes about love is a charlatan because it's all lies, isn't it? There are *no* happy endings. We *don't* all meet our Mr Darcys.'

Robyn reached a hand out and clasped Melissa's arm as a fat tear rolled down the journalist's pale cheek.

'I'm so sorry about what happened,' Robyn said,

'but you mustn't think you'll never meet the right man. Life wouldn't be worth living if you really believed that.'

'Well, I do believe it, okay?' Melissa gave a loud sniff and whipped her tear away with the back of her hand.

Robyn bit her lip. She wasn't sure what to say next but it would be worse if she didn't say anything at all. 'Do you want to talk about it?'

'About what?'

'About what happened.'

Melissa stared ahead into the green depths of a tree. 'What's there to tell? I was with Greg for two years. That might not seem long but, after a string of short-term boyfriends before that, it seemed like forever to me. I just assumed it would be forever too. We'd even talked about getting engaged but–'

'What?'

'He obviously had other ideas. Ideas which involved other women.'

'Oh, Melissa,' Robyn said.

'He left me for our neighbour,' Melissa said with a hollow laugh. 'I didn't even think he liked her! He was always complaining about her dreadful music.' She paused. 'He went round there one night about three months ago to have it out with her. I could hear them both shouting through the wall and then it went really quiet and he came stomping back, slamming our front door and cursing her.'

'So when did you find out they were seeing each other?'

Melissa closed her eyes. 'I came home early one day from work. I had a stinking cold and felt dreadful. I was going to go straight to bed but the neighbour –

Danielle her name is – had her music up at full volume so I went round and knocked on the door. There was no answer for ages so I tried the handle and shouted inside. When the music was turned off, Danielle appeared in the hallway. She was wearing a towel and her hair was dripping down her shoulders. When she saw me, this look of horror passed over her face and I knew something wasn't right but I didn't expect to see Greg there. I just wish he'd been wearing a towel too.'

Robyn's eyes widened at the revelation. 'What did you do?'

'I locked him out of our flat. I've left it since then. I couldn't stay there after that. I'm sleeping on a friend's sofa until things are sorted out.'

Robyn leaned forward. 'Things will get better,' she said.

'Will they?'

'Of course they will,' Robyn said. 'You know, I reached rock bottom too recently. I was with someone who made me unhappy and I didn't know how to get out of it. I felt as if my life was over and I'd never be happy again but then I met Dan and fell madly in love. We've got a daughter now.'

'Well, I'm very happy for you but that isn't going to happen for me, is it?' Melissa got up off the bench and walked away. Robyn followed her.

'It might seem like it won't happen but it will,' Robyn told her.

'You know that for a fact, do you? You're going to personally ensure my happiness, are you?'

'No of course not,' Robyn said, startled by Melissa's angry tone, 'but I wish I could.'

'Yeah, well wishing for happy ever afters doesn't

make them happen,' Melissa said, leaving Robyn hopelessly confounded as she strode off down the path.

Dan was in the kitchen at Horseshoe Cottage, trying to extricate Biscuit the terrier from a blue chiffon scarf that he'd somehow managed to pinch when nobody was looking and which was now wound around at least three of his legs.

Dan cursed under his breath as he struggled with his painful leg. First, dear old Moby had tipped his water bowl over, then Cassie had dropped one of her dolls down the back of the sofa and had howled until it had been rescued and now Biscuit appeared to be doing the dance of the seven veils with one of Robyn's favourite scarves. The morning had not been a relaxing one but at least Biscuit's antics were making Cassie laugh. She was sitting in her high chair at the other end of the kitchen, giggling in delight at the scene before her.

'Isn't he a naughty boy, Cassie? What are we going to do with him?' Dan said, finally extricating the little dog from the silky tangle he'd got himself into.

There was a knock at the door. Dan stood back up to full height, grabbed his crutches and went to see who it was. He wasn't expecting anybody but wasn't at all surprised to discover Higgins on the doorstep.

'I took the liberty of making you some soup, sir,' he said.

'Oh, Higgins – that is kind of you,' Dan said. 'Come in.'

Higgins walked into the kitchen and placed the covered pan on the cooker and then went over to where Cassie was and patted her red-gold curls.

'How are you, my little dear?' he said.

Cassie smiled up at him and the smile got broader as Higgins dug into his waistcoat pocket and produced a jelly baby.

'You do spoil her, Higgins,' Dan said.

'Not at all, sir,' he said. 'She's a little cherub. Now, let's get this soup on the go.'

'Don't worry about that,' Dan said.

'You sit down, sir. I've got it all under control.'

And Dan really was going to sit down because he knew Higgins wouldn't take no for an answer but something caught his eye out in the garden.

'Oh, no!' he cried.

Higgins joined him at the window. 'Is that hen meant to be in the vegetable patch eating all those lettuces?'

'Erm, no,' Dan said and the two of them made for the back door.

'I'm afraid there are two hens in there,' Higgins said a moment later and Dan recognised them instantly.

'Miss Bingley and Lydia,' he said. 'Those two are escape artists.' He did a quick head count of the ones left in the run to make sure there were no others missing and, when he looked back towards the vegetable patch, he saw the strange sight of Higgins chasing a hen around the rows of lettuce. Dan couldn't help but smile but his expression changed to that of a man impressed when Higgins managed to grab hold of Miss Bingley.

'Well done, Higgins!'

The butler walked calmly across the lawn, holding the hen tightly against his lime-green waistcoat and Dan watched as he returned the bird to its run before walking back and repeating the process with Lydia.

'I can't thank you enough,' Dan said. He hadn't even had a chance to drop his crutches and join in the chase.

'You're welcome, sir,' Higgins said before walking across the lawn back into the cottage as if nothing out of the ordinary had occurred.

But it was all too much for Cassie who suddenly burst into tears when Higgins and her father reappeared.

'What's wrong, little one?' Dan asked, leaning his crutches against the wall and picking Cassie up, cuddling her soft, warm body to him. 'You miss Mummy? I miss her too but she'll be home soon.'

Cassie pointed out of the window into the garden.

'Miss Bingley and Lydia are fine now. All safe. Higgins saved the day. *Again.*' He looked back to where Higgins had resumed heating up the soup on the Aga.

It was then that the phone rang. Dan popped Cassie into her high chair from where she sat watching Higgins whilst he went out to answer the phone.

'Dan?'

'Robyn!'

'Oh, it's so good to hear your voice.'

'Are you okay?' he asked.

'I've just had a really awful conversation with Melissa,' she said.

'The journalist?'

'Yes.'

'So I take it she isn't a full-blown Janeite yet?' Dan asked.

'We all thought it was going to be so easy,' Robyn

said with a sigh. 'Play her a few choice scenes and read her a few wonderful passages and she'd be converted in no time.'

'And that's not happening?'

'Not at all,' Robyn said. 'I can't seem to get through to her. Anyway, take my mind off it for a few minutes and tell me what's going on with you.'

'Oh, you know,' he said.

'I don't actually,' Robyn said, 'because I've never left you two alone before, have I?'

Dan laughed. 'Well, everything's fine.'

'Are you sure?' Robyn asked. 'Your voice sounds funny.'

'Does it?' Dan said.

'Yes,' Robyn said. 'It does.'

'Just a frog in my throat,' he said, clearing it. 'Cassie okay?'

'Of course,' he said, briefly recounting the tale of the doll down the sofa.

'And the hens?'

Dan cleared his throat again. 'All fine,' he said. He was most certainly not going to tell her about the hen escapade nor the exploding washing machine incident because he knew she'd only worry.

'I miss you guys so much,' she said.

'We miss you too,' he said.

'And the horses are okay? And Moby and Biscuit? Do watch Biscuit with my scarves,' she said. 'He's taken a liking to the sky-blue one recently for some reason.'

Dan winced.

'Dan?'

'Yes?'

'You *sure* everything's okay?'

'Soup is ready, sir,' Higgins's voice carried through to the hall.

'Is that Higgins?' Robyn said. 'What's he doing there?'

'Oh, he just made a big vat of soup and brought some over for us. Kind, eh?'

'Yes,' Robyn said. 'Perhaps he thought you'd be lonely.'

'That'll be it,' Dan said.

'Well, I suppose I'd better get back to it and make sure everyone's okay,' she said. 'I wish you were both here with me.'

'Me too, Dan said.

'I'll see you this evening, okay?'

'Bye, sweetheart,' he said. 'Love you!'

'Love you too – kiss Cassie for me.'

Dan hung up the phone and returned to the kitchen where Higgins was monitoring Cassie's progress at the table with her bowl of soup. Her cheeks and chin were orange but her eyes were bright with delight.

CHAPTER 13

Doris Norris was taking a photograph of the front of Lyme Park from across the lake when she saw Melissa approaching.

'Ah, my dear!' she called. 'Are you any good with cameras?'

'You want me to take a photo of you?'

'That would be absolutely marvellous,' Doris said, handing her tiny red camera to Melissa. 'Get Pemberley – I mean Lyme Park – in the background, won't you?' she said, smiling brightly.

Photo taken, Melissa returned the camera to Doris.

'Would you like me to take one of you?' Doris asked.

Melissa shook her head. 'No, thanks.'

Doris peered at her closely. 'You've been crying!' she said. 'Oh, my dear girl! Whatever is the matter?'

The tears started again and there was no stopping them this time. Doris took a step closer and hugged her.

'You just let it all out. Whatever it is. Let it all out.'

Doris wasn't sure how long she stood there holding Melissa but, when the young woman finally looked up, her face and eyes were red.

'Come and sit down,' Doris said and the two of them found a bench together.

'I'm sorry,' Melissa said. 'I'm making a real mess of everything this weekend.'

'No you're not,' Doris said.

'Everybody hates me, don't they?'

'What makes you say that?'

'I've seen the way they look at me when I'm

texting. Dame Pamela's always giving me "the look".'
Melissa rolled her eyes.

'Ah, well, that's just her little way if she thinks you're not giving Jane Austen one hundred percent of your attention,' Doris told her.

'And I haven't been. I've just been going through the motions.'

'What do you mean?' Doris asked, her head cocked to one side as she studied the journalist.

Melissa gave a sigh. 'I wanted to get away from it all,' she said, and then she told Doris the story she had told Robyn, her eyes misting with tears once more as the words tumbled out of her.

'Oh, my dear!' Doris said.

'So I grabbed this job, you see? And I've been rolling out all the awful clichés I could come up with about a bunch of Jane Austen nuts.' She looked up and caught Doris's eyes. 'Sorry,' she added.

'You think we're all nuts?'

Melissa's face took on a gentle look. 'No,' she said. 'Not anymore. Well, maybe just a little bit.' A tiny smile tickled the corners of her mouth. 'But I like you all. I really do and I think I'm slowly coming round to understanding what it is you all like about this writer so much.'

'Well, that's *wonderful!*' Doris said.

'I don't think I'm ever going to sit down and watch six episodes of *Pride and Prejudice* back to back or anything–'

'Now, don't be too rash,' Doris said. 'Give it time.'

Melissa smiled again. 'But I might give the book another go.'

Doris grabbed Melissa's hands in hers and squeezed them.

'And I'm going to rewrite my piece too,' she said. 'I'm going to make you all really proud of me.'

'I am proud of you already,' Doris said. 'Now, if we could only sort you out on the man front.'

Melissa shook her head. 'No, no,' she said. 'I think I'm beyond hope there.'

'What rubbish!' Doris said. 'You know, after my Henry died, I never thought of meeting anyone else. I really didn't want to. Henry and I were soul mates, you see. He was my first love and I was his.'

'But you did meet someone, didn't you?' Melissa said.

Doris gave a little smile. 'Maybe,' she said.

'What do you mean, *maybe*?' Melissa's eyes narrowed, her journalistic antennae on alert.

'Well, it's early days,' Doris said.

'But you're going to tell me he's absolutely perfect and that you're madly in love and that *I* can find true love too, aren't you?'

'I'm not going to say that at all,' Doris said, 'besides, I can't possibly tell if he's absolutely perfect although I very much doubt it. None of us are perfect, are we? Anyway, I only met him yesterday.'

Melissa frowned. 'Yesterday?' she said.

'Yes. At Chatsworth,' Doris said. 'In the sculpture gallery.'

A slight twitch pulled at Melissa's mouth and, suddenly, she was laughing and Doris joined in too, the sound carrying right across the lake.

'You see,' Doris said, once they'd managed to control themselves, 'wonderful things can happen when you're not looking for them. I wasn't thinking of meeting somebody when I went to Chatsworth but there he was, waiting for me. We've been swapping those text things ever since.'

Melissa's face settled into seriousness again. 'But I can't see *any*thing like that happening to me,' she said.

'Why do you say that?' Doris asked.

'Because it hasn't ever happened in the past,' she said.

'But don't you see – that makes it statistically more likely to happen in the future,' Doris told her. 'You've had all the rubbishy experiences whilst you're young enough to cope with them and get over them. Heaven only knows what wonderful man fate really has in store for your future!'

'I wish I had your optimism,' Melissa said.

'You don't need optimism,' Doris said. 'You just need a few more Jane Austen novels inside of you and *then* you'll believe in happy endings.'

'Ah! Is everybody here?' Dame Pamela said, clapping her hands and causing several tourists to turn and stare. It was four o'clock and their time at Lyme Park was drawing to a close after a day of delightful walks and a delicious lunch. 'How about a group photo at the spot where Elizabeth met Mr Darcy after his swim?'

'What a good idea,' Doris Norris said, smiling at Melissa who had cheered up immensely since their chat.

'Excellent,' Roberta agreed and she and Rose got into place.

'Oh, dear,' Dame Pamela suddenly said. 'Who's going to take the photograph?'

'Anne will,' Mrs Soames volunteered. 'Get hold of the camera, Anne. Don't stand there gormless and useless.'

Dame Pamela looked outraged on behalf of Annie. 'Mrs Soames,' she cried, 'I insist that Annie is actually *in* the photograph – not behind the camera taking it!' She then spotted a passer-by. 'Would you do the honours?' she asked, flinging the camera at the gentleman before he had a chance to protest.

All the gang were there. Katherine and Warwick had returned from their romantic walk up to Darcy's lake. Robyn, who was still getting over her earlier encounter with Melissa, had noticed that the journalist was smiling now and seemed to be very chummy with Doris.

They all jostled together with the grand face of Lyme Park behind them.

'Everybody say "Darcy"!' Dame Pamela sang and the photo was taken. 'I shall make sure everybody receives a copy and I'm sure Ms Berry would like one for her article, wouldn't you?'

Melissa nodded politely. 'Thank you.'

'Is that it, then?' Roberta asked, looking woeful.

'I'm afraid so,' Robyn said, 'although we'll be taking a look at the beautiful Derbyshire countryside on the way back to the hotel and we've got a wonderful tea to look forward to before heading home.'

'I don't want to leave,' Roberta said. 'I wonder if anybody would notice if I moved into a very small room in the house.'

'What a *silly* thing to say,' Mrs Soames said. 'Now, can you all get out of the way so I can get a photo of the house? I don't want you all in it.'

'Charming!' Rose said.

'*So* rude!' Roberta said. Nevertheless, the group and other tourists moved aside so that the formidable

Mrs Soames could get her perfect shot.

Doris shook her head but she was smiling. 'For a reader of Jane Austen, she hasn't really got a great command of the English language, has she? You'd think she'd have learned a few words that would make her more affable, wouldn't you?'

'And amiable,' Robyn said, relishing the use of one of her favourite Austen words.

Melissa, who was listening and watching intently, smiled at the exchanges and everybody watched as Mrs Soames walked backwards across the lawn to enable her tiny camera to get all of the house in.

'She's getting a bit close to the water, isn't she?' Rose said. 'Shouldn't somebody warn–'

But it was too late. Mrs Soames, her camera pressed up against her face, took one step back too many and, with an almighty splash, landed in the lake, her huge bottom and bosom sending a gallon of water up into the air.

Screams and cries came from the crowd gathered which had swollen far beyond the Purley Hall holidaymakers now.

'Somebody *do* something!' Dame Pamela cried, clutching her hands in front of her as Mrs Soames continued to splash in the shallows. Dame Pamela caught Warwick's eye but he didn't need to be asked because he'd already kicked his boots off and was heading towards the water, leaping straight in.

It wasn't deep but Mrs Soames was flailing around so much that Warwick was soon fully immersed himself.

'Get me out of here, you stupid man!' Mrs Soames cried and Warwick grabbed her round her substantial middle and did his best to shift her onto dry land where Annie and Robyn helped to pull her out.

'Oh, Mother!' Annie said, her expression torn between anxiety and amusement.

'Warwick!' Katherine was there to help him out of the water and gasped as she realised that his white shirt was now transparent. He was soon surrounded by a crowd of female tourists who were snapping him with their cameras and filming the moment on their phones.

'My hero,' Katherine said.

'Well, you did say you wanted to see me in a lake,' he said, shaking his wet hair and they both laughed.

CHAPTER 14

It was a rather subdued Mrs Soames that got into the minibus after drying off as best as she could and getting changed with the help of Robyn. She refused to get out again when they reached the viewpoint for Stanage Edge where Keira Knightley playing Elizabeth Bennet had communed most beautifully with nature.

'She's afraid of finding any more water,' Roberta said with a naughty grin as they all trooped off the bus.

Warwick was bare-chested underneath a jacket which the minibus driver, Mr Allsop, had lent him. It was far too small and afforded the ladies quite a sight.

Katherine teased him about it. 'You're lapping up all this attention, aren't you?'

'I was just doing my duty. That's all,' he said, giving her a wink and grinning as he caught Roberta taking a photo of him with her mobile phone.

Mrs Soames had fared less well in the wardrobe department, wearing a designer raincoat that belonged to Dame Pamela and which had been kept on the bus in case of showers.

'I do hope she doesn't stretch it,' Dame Pamela said to Robyn as she walked across the countryside in the walking boots which Higgins had insisted upon. 'It's a limited edition.'

Robyn fought a smile as she remembered the sight of a sopping Mrs Soames emerging from the lake. Of course, she'd been terribly concerned at the time but no harm had come to the older lady. In fact, her cold dunk seemed to have subdued her which was really rather pleasant for everyone else.

All too soon, it was time to return to Bakewell where a sumptuous tea had been laid out for them. There were scones and fruit breads, Bakewell puddings, flapjacks, cakes and an endless supply of tea.

Melissa Berry was sitting next to Robyn and cleared her throat.

'Robyn?'

'Yes?'

'I want to apologise for before,' she said.

'Oh?'

Melissa nodded. 'I was really rude and I know you were only trying to help me.'

'It's okay. Don't mention it.' Robyn still felt upset about the incident and returned to her scone.

'No – listen. *Please.*'

Robyn gave Melissa her full attention. 'What is it?'

'I want you to help me.'

'Help you?' Robyn said. 'How can I help you?'

'You're a Jane Austen fan, right?'

'Of course,' she said.

'Then I need you to help me with this article I'm writing. I'd like to really make an impact with it – use some good quotes, some really emotive stuff that will stir the readers and help spread the word about her to non-believers like me.'

'Really?'

'Yes – really,' Melissa said. 'Will you help me?'

Robyn bit her lip but she didn't need to think about it for long and nodded enthusiastically. 'I'd *love* to help you,' she said, looking forward to telling her little group the good news.

'Great!' Melissa said and the two of them smiled at

one another, the beginnings of a friendship blossoming over afternoon tea.

An hour later, Robyn and Dame Pamela waved Katherine and Warwick off for their journey back to Oxfordshire.

'Come and visit us at Hawk's Hill soon,' Katherine called to Robyn.

'We will!' she called back.

Then they watched as Mrs Soames levered herself into her car with Doris in the back seat. Annie followed with the bags and, after putting them into the boot, approached Robyn and Dame Pamela.

'I can't thank you enough for all you've done,' she said.

'It's been a real pleasure to meet you,' Dame Pamela said, squeezing Annie's hands in her diamond-clad ones. 'Now, you will join us at Purley for Christmas, won't you?'

Annie took a deep breath. 'Well, I–'

'Oh, *do* say yes!' Robyn said. 'I can't imagine one of our get-togethers without you now.'

Annie beamed a smile. 'And I'd hate to miss one,' she said.

'Good,' Robyn said. 'Take care of yourself.'

Annie nodded just as her mother honked the car horn.

'We haven't got all day, Anne!' she said, poking her head out of the window.

'She'll never change, will she?' Dame Pamela said.

'I fear not,' Annie said and they watched as she got into the car beside her mother. Doris blew kisses at them and they began their journey back to the Cotswolds.

It was ten minutes later when Mrs Soames caught sight of a grinning Doris Norris in her rear view mirror.

'What have *you* got to smile about?' she asked disgruntled.

'I've met somebody,' Doris said.

Mrs Soames made a dismissive sound. 'What are you talking about? We don't meet people at *our* age.'

'Well, *I* have,' Doris said and she stared out of the window, her smile lighting up her face until she reached home.

'Melissa's left already, hasn't she?' Dame Pamela said, turning to Robyn at the front of the hotel.

'Her taxi for the station came as soon as soon as tea was over,' she said.

'Yes. She said she had to go but I wanted to talk to her some more. She was rather a tricky character, wasn't she? It's a shame she didn't really get into the spirit of the weekend, isn't it?'

'Oh, I'm not so sure,' Robyn said.

'What do you mean?' Dame Pamela asked.

'I think she's beginning to come round to our way of thinking.'

'You do?'

'I really do, and she's asked for my input with the article she's writing so I don't think we've got any worries there. She really did like us all.'

Dame Pamela sighed in satisfaction. 'What a dear girl. I liked her as soon as I saw her, you know.'

Robyn grinned. 'Come on,' she said. 'We've got to round up Rose and Roberta and get going ourselves.'

'Yes,' Dame Pamela said. 'Like Elizabeth Bennet

I am "wild to be at home", aren't you?'

Robyn thought of Dan and Cassie and Horseshoe Cottage. 'Oh, yes!' she said.

CHAPTER 15

Robyn sighed with relief at her first sighting of Horseshoe Cottage. She'd not even been away for three whole days but it seemed like a lifetime to her.

The minibus had dropped her at the end of the unmade road that led to her home on the Purley Hall estate and Robyn walked down it in the fading evening light, the last of the day's swallows screeching overhead.

Opening the little gate and dragging her suitcase along the path, she brushed her fingers lightly on the horseshoe door knocker before turning the handle.

'Hellooooo!' she called into the house.

'Robyn!' Dan called from the kitchen.

'Dan!' she cried, catching sight of her husband as he appeared in the doorway on crutches. 'What on earth's happened? Are you okay?'

'I'm fine – totally fine. I just got kicked by Winter when she got spooked.'

'But you're on crutches,' Robyn said, quite unnecessarily.

'Just to stop things from getting worse,' Dan said. 'Got to keep my weight off this leg.'

'Oh, my God! Why didn't you tell me? How have you been coping with Cassie? Is that why Higgins was here? How have you been walking the dogs and–'

'I've coped, okay? I'm not a total invalid. I've just had to be a bit inventive about how I do things.'

'But I would have come home if I'd known.'

'I know you would have and that's why I didn't tell you,' he said with a smile.

'Oh, Dan! I feel awful.'

'Don't feel awful,' he said. 'Come here and give me a kiss.'

Robyn moved towards him and felt herself glowing with warmth in his embrace. How she had missed that, she thought.

'I never want to leave here again. Not ever,' she said a moment later, placing her hands on his chest and looking up into his handsome face.

'You don't have to,' he told her.

Robyn sighed. 'Well, Pammy's already talking about the next trip. She wants to see the place where they shot the interiors for Pemberley in the 1995 adaptation.'

Dan smiled. 'Tell her she'll have to take somebody else's wife next time.'

Robyn laughed. 'Well, I'll probably end up going but I won't like it!'

'Yes you will,' Dan said, 'and it will do you good. Everyone should get away from time to time. It makes you appreciate home all the more.'

'I don't need to go away to appreciate what I've got right here,' Robyn said, cuddling into him and sighing in contentment. 'In fact, there's something I've been wanting to talk to you about. Something that would keep me at home for the foreseeable future.'

'Really? What's that?' he asked.

She gazed up at him and smiled and the twinkle in his bright eyes told her that he understood her perfectly.

'Let's go upstairs,' he said.

'Can you make it on those things?' she asked, concern etched across her face as she looked at his crutches.

'Trust me – I can make it,' he said, giving her a wink before they headed up the stairs together, looking in on the sleeping Cassie and kissing her goodnight before walking into their own room and closing the door behind them.

It was good to be back at Hawk's Hill. It really was a special place to come home to, Katherine thought as they drove up the driveway and gazed at the honey-coloured Georgian exterior, the sun setting behind the gold-green fields beyond.

After parking the car and unloading the boot, they opened the front door to be greeted by the cats, Freddie and Fitz. Chrissie, who'd been sitting the house, had left a little note by the phone, saying she'd made them some supper. Katherine smiled at the thoughtfulness of her friend.

The heaps of books were still waiting to be sorted in each of the rooms but Katherine wasn't thinking about those as she walked through the house and up the stairs, her hand gently stroking the warm wood of the banister rail.

She knew where she was going: to the little room next door to the master bedroom and, when she entered it, she felt the warmth of the day still lingering within its walls. The view from the window took in the great sweep of lawn at the back of the house and the herbaceous borders filled with roses, lilies and delphiniums. It was a beautiful room. An empty room. The room which she'd hadn't been able to stop thinking about since her conversation with Robyn at Chatsworth.

'Katherine?' Warwick's voice called from the landing. 'Where are you?'

'I'm in here,' she said and he soon joined her by the window.

'What are you doing in here?' he asked, resting his hands on her shoulders.

'Just thinking,' she said.

'Oh, yeah?' he said. 'What about?'

'About–' she paused and turned to face him, looking up into his dark eyes. 'About how we're going to use this room.'

'Guest bedroom, I thought you'd said.'

She shook her head. 'Not next to ours.'

Warwick nodded. 'Where are you going with this, Cherry? I know you're going somewhere, aren't you?'

'I think you know where this is going.'

'Do I?'

'Well, you've been dropping hints about it ever since we got married,' she said.

'You mean?' His eyes widened and his face filled with a wonderful light. '*Katherine!*'

She smiled at him, feeling his joy mingling with her own and growing so rapidly that she couldn't help but laugh.

'But what about your work?' he asked, stroking her hair.

She took a deep breath. 'Now, I'm not saying I'm going to give up work,' she told him earnestly. 'I don't think I ever could do that but, right now, that doesn't seem so important to me.' She drew him closer to her until their bodies were touching, warm, comforting and natural. '*This* is what's important to me – you and me and a family.'

Warwick bent his head to kiss her. 'You don't know how happy I am to hear you say that,' he told her.

'I do,' she said, resting her head on his chest and hearing the beating of his heart. 'You know Robyn wants to try for another baby?'

'Does she?'

Katherine nodded. 'And I can't have her getting *too* far ahead in the baby stakes, can I?'

Warwick laughed and squeezed her closer to him. 'I love it when you're competitive,' he said and the two of them stood there together by the sash window, kissing and smiling and kissing again as they thought with great joy about their future.

ABOUT THE AUTHOR

Victoria Connelly was brought up in Norfolk and studied English literature at Worcester University before becoming a teacher. After getting married in a medieval castle in the Yorkshire Dales and living in London for eleven years, she moved to rural Suffolk where she lives with her artist husband and a mad Springer spaniel and ex-battery hens.

Her first novel, *Flights of Angels*, was published in Germany and made into a film. Victoria and her husband flew out to Berlin to see it being filmed and got to be extras in it.

Several of her novels have been Kindle bestsellers.

If you'd like to sign up for her newsletter about future releases, visit her website www.victoriaconnelly.com.

She's also on Facebook and Twitter @VictoriaDarcy

BOOKS BY VICTORIA CONNELLY

Austen Addicts Series

A Weekend with Mr Darcy
The Perfect Hero
- published in the US as Dreaming of Mr Darcy
Mr Darcy Forever
Christmas with Mr Darcy
Happy Birthday, Mr Darcy
At Home with Mr Darcy

Other Fiction

The Rose Girls
The Secret of You
A Summer to Remember
Wish You Were Here
The Runaway Actress
Molly's Millions
Flights of Angels
Irresistible You
Three Graces
It's Magic (A compilation volume: Flights of Angels,
Irresistible You and Three Graces)
Christmas at the Cove
A Dog Called Hope

Short Story Collections

One Perfect Week and other stories
The Retreat and other stories
Postcard from Venice and other stories

Non-fiction

Escape to Mulberry Cottage
A Year at Mulberry Cottage
Summer at Mulberry Cottage

Children's Adventure

Secret Pyramid
The Audacious Auditions of Jimmy Catesby

The following titles are
also available as audio books

A Dog Called Hope
The Secret of You
Christmas at the Cove
A Weekend with Mr Darcy
Christmas with Mr Darcy
Happy Birthday, Mr Darcy
At Home with Mr Darcy
Molly's Millions
The Rose Girls
Escape to Mulberry Cottage

Printed in Great Britain
by Amazon

28284281R00074